There are too many people that I would like to thank. Family, friends and even the universe for making this happen. For loving and supporting my dreams and pushing me to do this. Shalise Jackson you're amazing. Mom, Jeff, Grandma Jan, Grandpa Chuck, Aunt Syl, Uncle Ray and Jason. Sarrah, Justin, Kyleigh, Kaycie, Leger, Channing and Marley. Travis, Stephanie, Maddy, Charlotte and Ryan. Thank you all for your love and support.

Rosa, Aidan, Marylou, Mercy and Bella, thank you for being so amazing and keeping my spirits up. Amy & Michelle, thank you for believing in me when nobody else did.

Shane & Kjerstin thank you. I could say it a million times and it still won't seem to be enough. Everything that you have done for me has helped get me here and I am eternally grateful.

A huge thank you to Don and the entire Scales family for being the amazing humans that you are. For loving and supporting me and believing in me. It means more to me than anything.

I am sure there are others, so I will just have to thank you in the next book!

D1550886

This book is dedicated to anyone who has a dream and isn't afraid to follow that dream and remember: if you come across a bit of magic, its best not to ask questions. 12-13-14

The Morning Glories

It was a heartrending, cheerless day when that old eclectic

lamp got yanked from the table and shattered into one hundred and

twenty-three pieces. Yes, I counted.

Grandma was a handful after all, going from room to room and

unplugging everything. Finding anything that could fit in the palm

of her frail hands and placing them inside the lamp. It was a

medium sized lamp with a clear, vase-like base and it had a single

luminescent light bulb with a simple light purple lamp shade. Her

random knick-knacks that she would find on her adventures, her

adventures being the many, many rooms in her house that had life's

greatest treasures—to her—buried in the drawers and on the shelves.

She has found this same, *I Love Lucy* pendant forty-three times and

always places it at the tippy top.

When grandma goes to sleep at night and I can hear the slight

hissing of her oxygen tube as it feeds her lungs, I know that she is

asleep…past REM stage. I walk into the living room and remove the purple lamp shade—reminiscent of the morning glories when they first peak open their petals at the arrival of the sun—and begin removing all of grandma's treasures and then I hide them once more throughout the house. All so she can go on another adventure the next day and find it once more. It may seem cruel, letting her find the same things day after and then putting them back night after night, but for her it is the first time she is finding them, and it makes her happy.

You see, grandma had dementia. And although I was named *Charles* after my grandpa, her late husband, she had renamed me *Poodle*. Yes, Poodle. Nobody knows where she came up with that name, but she insisted it was mine. Her weathered, pale blue eyes would light up when she would say my name.

"Oh Poodle, have you ever spoken to the morning glories?" She would ask elatedly. I was not about to take any of that away from her.

It seemed like an easy enough task moving grandma in with me after grandpa had died, he took such good care of her in the beginning stages of her dementia. But then he became weary and she got out of hand. And on the final night of grandpa's life, she got out of the house...or so he thought. Grandpa awoke to an empty bed as a gentle breeze blew through the open back door. He searched the fields as the invigorating winter winds whipped him into submission, slowing him to a crawl.

"I'll just rest here." He must have thought as he posted up next to the fence post covered in morning glories and took his final breath. Only grandma never actually went outside. She simply opened the door before heading into the guest bathroom and falling asleep in the claw foot porcelain bathtub. That was where I found her when I arrived early the next morning.

His death was easy. When grandma and I went to look for him, it didn't take long for us to find him where we found him: grandma's second favorite spot on their property where the morning glories grew. He was posted up with his back against the fence post, frozen, next to the morning glories.

"Charles...have you spoken to the morning glories?" She softly asked. It was her way of saying goodbye. Goodbye to a man she had been married to for over sixty years, but now, had no idea who he was and what his connection was to her. She only remembered his name. he looked peaceful and I didn't cry for him, just as he knew I wouldn't.

I have two great brothers that loved grandma as much as I did, but they both have families and couldn't take on such an ardent task. My two sisters, awful as they are, didn't even show up to grandpa's funeral. They merely enquired as to what, if anything, he left to them in his will—nothing. Nothing but two personal letters explaining that the materialistic possessions which run their lives will not pay for missed memories and that although they had given up on grandma and grandpa, they still love them and remember as they once were when they were young. Knee high to a pig's eye, picking strawberries in the field, eyes full of adventure and hearts so uncontaminated.

Relationships in my family are tumultuous to say the least. What was once a close-knit family, like *The Brady Bunch*, was now scattered to the winds. Everything was great in our lives until the day after my twenty-eighth birthday. That was the day that my two sisters had conspired against the rest of us to try and ram our vehicle into the river. Mom, dad, grandma, grandpa and I were just leaving the restaurant—where we enjoyed a fervent evening with all the family—when my sisters, driving in the car behind us, rammed our vehicle as we crossed over the single lane bridge. I thought it was an accident—their striking us—but then it happened again and again. The look of terror in moms' eyes as she just looked back, in dismay, to see her daughters...her own flesh and blood trying to push us all over the wall into the river. Luckily, I was driving. I had taken courses in defensive driving and knew how to get out of that situation. They had just sniggered it off as a joke and couldn't understand why we were all so visibly shaken and upset.

Earlier that day at grandpa and grandma's, mom had loosely talked about how her and dad changed their life insurance policies, upping them to $750,000.

"Enough to make sure that you kids are well taken care of after we pass..." Mom had said.

Apparently, that was all that she needed to say before my two sisters decided to do what they did. I never forgave them for their actions that day. Mom and dad, humble and magnanimous as they are, say that they had forgiven them, but I know they didn't. Grandma and grandpa meant *everything* to mom; they were her only parents, and she was their only child. I bonded more than any of my siblings with grandpa and grandma. It's like our hearts were in sync and we spoke each other's language. It's difficult to describe, but when you love someone so deep, so unconditionally, there is a deeper language than the one you speak. It is a language that you can't audibly speak or hear, but a language that you *feel* in your heart and in your soul.

Mom and dad had decided, against my wishes, not to report them to the police. There was no way to really explain to the insurance company how my vehicle acquired the damage to the back, so dad paid for the repairs…out of pocket. There was a long, somber silence, coming from my sisters' end. Their attempt to push us all in the river—I hesitate to use the term attempted murder—had failed and they were mad. They were mad that *we* were mad…that *I* was mad. I was more hurt than anything. Not a physical hurt, but an emotional hurt. The scar that formed on my heart that day in the form of feeling shame for my two sisters who, up until that point, I never thought could hurt a fly. So, you can *imagine* their resentment when mom removed their names from the insurance policies and the will. I had concerns that this might make them harder to harm us, but mom didn't seem to think so.

"What they did was horrible…but nobody would be stupid enough to try that twice…right?" Mom said with hints of sudden remorse.

I wasn't convinced, not even for a minute. However, I played along with mom and her delusion, whatever helped her moved pass it and move on with her life. Dad on the other hand, well, he bought a gun.

Chapter Two

"Poodle, don't follow your dreams…follow your heart." Grandma said that to me once as she studied my eyes, cautiously. She knew me so well. Knew that my dreams consisted of being a pirate on the open seas with a treasure chest buried underneath a giant red X on a deserted island with golden sand and palm trees that swayed in the ocean breeze, its location annotated on a flimsy map made of parchment.

Early on in life, it was poetry that saved me from all my prepubescent torment. I turned to expressing myself solely through words, smashed eternally in the pages of a book. I once slept on a train next to a man with dark eyes and a fedora. As I slept soundly, he read the pages of my deepest of feelings. He must have liked what he read because he shook me awake, abruptly, and introduced himself as Ripp Carnegie, a music producer for Sony records. My heart told me to write music, so that is what I did. Seven years ago, next Monday, and now my words are highly sought after. I still wish I could be a pirate.

I am now thirty years old, in the best shape of my life and divorced. My ex-wife, Raven, thought that I was overreacting when I stopped communicating with my sisters, with whom she was *extremely* close to. "They're like the sisters I never had," she told me on countless occasions, usually when they had surprised her with a gift or a sister's bracelet charm.

"Yeah, they tried to kill you guys, but they didn't. are you going to punish them forever? Raven contemptuously asked.

I felt like I knew my wife, and I knew those weren't her words, they were the words of my sisters. They were bewitching Raven to try and fix things with me, and Raven was hypnotized by the ensnare of sisterhood. She sided with them in the end and five long months later we were officially divorced—her doing. Thank God she signed a prenuptial agreement before we took our declarations; I had to protect my residue and my capital that I earned without her. At our wedding, grandma even told Raven that she wasn't right for me.

"Mark my words, Crow, you are nothing but trouble!" Grandma said to her. Raven immediately fired back.

"My name is Raven...not Crow!" Great wedding, I tell you.

Grandma's procession was like a dirge but beautiful song and everyone whose lives were impacted in some way by Grandma were there to pay their respects. Mom had grandma cremated and had her ashes sealed in a ceramic urn adorned in morning glory's painted in colors the rainbow hasn't even created yet. She placed grandma on her mantle, next to grandpa's urn.

Every Sunday, as we would have dinner at mom and dad's house, I would look around the room and be pleased to see my brothers Shawn and Trevor and their families all present. My awful sisters, Tillie and Enzi had always refused to show; probably out of disgrace for themselves and their actions. Mom had insisted that she and dad were over their failed attempt at a quick inheritance, but dad always felt the need to remind the two of them that he had purchased a gun and he kept it close by…always. I also think they were afraid to face Shawn, Trevor and maybe even me. I, after all, am the success story of our family and have made an undersized fortune by selling my songs to big artists that have made millions of dollars from me. Although I only received a fraction of what of what they earned, it was a very handsome living. I would freely give money to any of my family who asked, but that stopped when they tried to push us in the river.

After looking around the room, my eyes darting back and forth like an inundated man with PTSD in a large crowd, I would drag my eyes over to grandma and grandpa, sitting on the mantle, voiceless everlastingly. Two years had passed, and I had finally had enough. After everyone had gone to bed, I drunkenly decided to take grandma and grandpa's ashes from the urns on the mantle and replaced them with soil from the garden. I kept them with me always and, at times, I even felt their presence. More grandma than grandpa, but still, I felt something.

"Mom..." I softly asked while we were having lunch, talking about the latest song that I sold to a singer who now had her first number one hit, "...instead of selling grandpa and grandma's house...can I buy it?" She looked at me, void, eyes blue like the ocean but relieved.

"You don't have to do that, Charles." She said.

"I'm happiest when I am there mom. I need to do this...for me." I said as I paused to gather my words. "To feel closer to grandma and grandpa." Mom knew that I had the means and was happy to see it stay in our family.

"Yes…" was all that she had said, I could tell that she wanted to say more but the look on her face said everything. It said everything and nothing all at the same time and it made me apprehensive but appreciative.

Years earlier, before they died, grandma and grandpa took out a second mortgage against the house and mom just asked that I pay that remaining balance and then it was mine. After thirty days, $418,000 dollars and multiple sleepless nights, mom transferred the deed into my name. I contentedly moved in, ready to start the next chapter of my life. With the help of mom, dad and Shawn and Trevor, it took just three hours to fully moved in. I opted to sell most of my furniture and keep all of grandpa and grandmas. I wanted their house to remain, in most part, the same as I remembered it in my memories from when I was a young boy. When grandma would tell me magical stories about the morning glories as we would sit next to the fireplace and cup our hands around mugs of hot chocolate, and how they will speak to you if you believe.

That night, when everyone toasted my new house with the clinking of wine glasses, we all took to the fields behind the house. The fresh scent of strawberries as they floated on puffs of air and lightning bugs illuminated the sky in arbitrary bursts of radiance, making this place the magical haven I knew it to be. I had counted, every time I went to the house after they both had died, that there were exactly twenty-three morning glories in bloom. Over the span of a few months, no new ones budded or bloomed, just twenty-three. I thought the house was ailing, despite the smell of fresh strawberries in the air and the magical brilliancy of lightning bugs. I decided, once everyone left and I was all alone with my thoughts, that it was the soil beneath the morning glories that was sick, so I did the only feasible thing I thought would cure the ailment: I deposited grandma and grandpas' ashes in the soil, next to the roots.

I woke up from a deep slumber the next morning just before the sun would peak its rays over the hills to a soft whisper in my ear.

"Charles, have you spoken to the morning glories?" My eyes shot open as I turned my head towards the window. I didn't see anyone, didn't hear anyone...no more voice. I turned on the bedside lamp and was taken back to see a midnight lavender colored morning glory had been placed on the nightstand, on top of my note pad with the number *24* circled. What could this mean, I thought to myself as I gazed out the window, holding the morning glory up to my nose and inhaling deeply; it smelled like grandma. The sun was just peaking over the hills as I faintly heard a rooster crow. I could feel the sorrow and exhilaration in the roosters' crow, thankful that he had survived another night, fox free. I turned on the coffee pot and poured myself a cup of coffee—black as coal—and stepped outside to welcome the day. I studied the trellis that held the twenty-three morning glories and was taken back. Upon closer inspection, I counted twenty-four.

Chapter Three

"Always trust your gut, Poodle; it is the only thing that is with you every minute of every day for your entire life." I sat in the chair next to the lead-paned window, next to a box that I hadn't unpacked yet, holding the post card that grandma sent me from her last trip, Catalina Island. She sent me the post card that had those words emblazoned, but nothing else. I felt her presence last night as I drifted off to sleep, in her bed. The blanket around my feet even tightened, as if I had been tucked in. Grandma used to tuck my feet in when I was but a child to protect me from my overactive, child-like imagination. Only on this night, I didn't open my eyes or even move a muscle. I even made sure that my breathing remained impartial, anything not run her off. Maybe she just wanted to be a physical entity again.

Some nights I even leave all her treasure openly lying around the house, unhidden. I miss her. All the advice that she would freely give to me in the form of a conundrum, like words of alliteration. It pains me to think that I brushed them off as dementia ramblings at first, but soon after her death they began to make more and more sense.

"There's my favorite song writer…" Ripp jubilantly shouted over his Bluetooth is his car, I could hear the wind whipping by him as he drove with the top down. I let out a sigh. "So, listen Charles…I have an idea…," He excitedly triumphed. I quickly interrupted.

"Ripp, I'm not interested in singing my own songs…what else do you have for me?" I asked.

"Charles, you have such a timeless voice, we could…" He paused, clearing his throat, "…you could make millions." I was silent. "I know that you are happy with how much you currently make just by selling your songs…which are beautiful I might add…" He said as he sensed my exhaustion. I was tired of having the same conversations about the same things, just like when I was married to Raven. "…But if you just consider it, I'll be happy. Just mull it over." He said. "Also, I have an up-and-coming artist who needs a song about forgiveness, four weeks?" He asked.

"I will have it to you in one." I told him.

"I look forward to it; you are looking to make $37,000 off it." He said as he hung up the phone.

I sat there looking out the window as a gentle breeze blew in a familiar smell of memories from the past, strawberries, fresh cut grass, sugar snap peas and morning glories. "Trust your gut." Grandma said. Deep down I *do* want to sing my own songs, but there is always the fear that it will not convey the way that I want it to, it may not reach the people it is intended for. The post card, the smells, even the phone call from Ripp, I felt like it was grandma's doing. "Well, I guess I can at least consider his offer." I thought to myself.

I dozed off in the chair next to the window as that familiar, proverbial smell gently caressed my face.

"Charles, have you ever spoken to the morning glories?" The breeze asked. I slowly opened my eyes; I smelled grandma nearby. I got up to follow the smell but was surprised to find that a lavender blue morning glory had been placed in my palm. I did not even realize I had been holding it. I stared at it, awestruck, as it *finally* hit me like a freight train: the riddle.

"Have you ever spoken to the morning glories?" I quietly repeated to myself under my breath as I stood next to the window. The breeze blew the morning glory out of my palm.

I walked outside, following the smells of grandma. The smell led me to the place my gut told me it would; the place where I buried grandma and grandpa's ashes: underneath the trellis which held the morning glories. I stared, fixated on the vines that wrapped around the trellis as I counted every bloom. "Twenty-seven..." I said. "...Twenty-seven morning glories in full bloom." They were the colors of memories and purple sunsets over rolling hills; I stared at the biggest flower, the one that appeared to be staring back at me.

"Have you ever spoken to the morning glories?" I asked. I was transfixed on the profound purple hues that seemed to hypnotize me. A breeze blew an indistinct message pass my ears. I scooted closer to the bloom and turned my face, pressing my ear up to the flower. I do not know what I had expected, and I *must* have looked fanatical as I tolerantly waited to hear something, anything. But all I heard was the gentle buzzing of a bee.

I refused to accept that, amongst all the magic in this magical place, it would *not* be selfish to ask for just a little more magic. The breeze blew once more as I scooted closer to the bloom. A faint message began to occupy my ears, but this time it was perceptibly comprehensible. It was grandma's voice.

"Took you long enough, Poodle." She said as I began to suppurate. It was her; I just knew it. I was dirge for so many reasons; I was joyful and miserable. I felt like I was in a sinister place in my life and every single day that had passed by, I felt like I was losing my grip on actuality. It is true that when I am in these types of places, some of my most paramount work comes from it. But every time that I would fall, it would be even harder to get back up.

"Grandma, is that you?" I asked, uncertainly but certainly. I knew it was her; I wanted it to be her. The truth is that I miss her so much. It hurts how much I miss her. Only I did not comprehend just how much I treasured and required her until after she had died. isn't that always how it is?

"Of course, it's me Poodle, who else would it be?" I was so overjoyed that I had to pinch myself. How is this possible? What kind of sorcery is this, I thought to myself? I knew she would not answer the questions that were floating on the open sea of my mind. She would always tell me that if you stumble upon a bit of magic, it is best not to ask questions, just must believe.

"Grandma, I miss you so much. I need you. I don't know what I am doing anymore." I pleaded. I was always more of a strong-willed person, but as of late I had no idea what path I was on. I was at a fork in the crossroads and I did not know which way to go; left or right.

"Oh Poodle, we don't have much time. Just remember this: there is a crack in everything, it's how the light shines in." She prophetically said. I took a step back and stared at the barricade of morning glories that all seemed to be angled towards me, like she was speaking to me through all of them.

"Another puzzle?" I asked. I waited, but there was no response. "We don't have much time…" I echoed. Maybe this line of communication has a time limit or something. I looked down at the watch that securely hugged my wrists, reading a doleful six o' clock. I had to have been standing out in front of the morning glories for at least thirty minutes. I thanked the flowers as I grabbed the watering can and deluged them graciously.

I went back inside and put logs on the fire and fixed myself a hot cup of cocoa, spiked with just a bit of rum. I thought to myself as I sat in the chair and looked at the morning glory that I had brought in with me. I held it by the stalk and rolled it between my fingertips, making it twirl like a wedding dress. "My first question tomorrow…" I began to say to the flower, "…will be to ask what the rules of communicating are." I looked at the flower and studied it, anticipating a response. We stared at each other as I sipped cocoa and, for the first time since I lost grandma, I felt creativity begin to flow through my veins once more.

"A song about forgiveness." I thought to myself as the words began to pour out of my mind faster than I could write them down. I finished writing the composition as I felt a sense of accomplishment draining from my pores. I read it and then re-read it to the flower as if it were my audience. "This may just be one of the best things I have ever written." I told the flower as I closed my notebook and watched the embers dance in the stone fireplace. The flames of blue, red, orange and green gave me hope and respite. "There's a crack in everything, it's how the light shines in." I said to myself as I laid down and pulled the weighty blanket over me, tucking myself in the way grandma used to do.

Chapter Four

"Poodle, if you see a charmer, then nearby there is bound to be a snake." As I twirled the lemon-herbed angel hair pasta onto the tines of my fork—the mirror of my family in the reflection—everyone was cheerfully engaged in banter. I was void, staring off into a vast nothing with just the thoughts in my head and an empty gaze which painted on my face a canvas of concern. As I looked pass everyone, thinking of grandma, they all began to appear as nothing more than colorful blurs.

"Where are you? Earth to Charles!" Trevor said as mom shook me, jolting me back to a state of reality.

"Mmhmm…sorry, what?" I asked as I looked around the room, all eyes on me.

"…I said…" Trevor began to huff, "…that Raven sent me a text message today asking how you are doing and where you would be tonight." I looked at him with a confused look plastered across my face.

"Why does she care? Isn't she with John or James or whatever his name is?" I asked. My bearing and my blasé attitude conveyed to everyone just how much I had moved on and didn't care. Ant it was true, I did move on I truly didn't care anymore. I know deep down that that I still care, and it was evident that Raven had moved on with her fastidious number of rebound lovers. I put all my time and effort into work *and* remodeling the antiquated electrical and plumbing at grandma and grandpas' house. As far as I could tell, Raven put her time and effort into all men who showed her the slightest amount of interest.

Trevor has always loved to ruffle my feathers, so he would always tell me every time that Raven got in a new relationship. "She is with James." Trevor brusquely said. "…But…she just changed her relationship status to 'it's complicated', which I think means she is looking for a new flavor of the month." I looked at him as my face perceptibly went flush, mom reached over and grabbed my arm and smiled. Deep down, I still cared. Hell, I was married to her. But she has been tainted by the clutch of sisterhood, something she had always craved, having grown up as an only child. But she was brutally loyal to Tillie and Enzi, and I know they would not approve of her texting Trevor, especially because Trevor had written them off and wouldn't give either of them the time of day.

"What is her number?" I asked.

"Her phone number?" Trevor confoundedly asked. I looked at him with a disgusted look on my face and fake wretched, quite dramatically.

"God no! If I even thought about talking to her, grandma would haunt me." I said as I laughed.

"Damn right she would." Mom said.

"I mean her number, like how many men since the divorce?" I clarified.

"Ohhhh…" Trevor sighed. "I think James is number three." I rolled my eyes at his answer, why did I even ask him that question, I thought to myself. The rest of the evening went by fast, but it was enjoyable as always.

As mom and dad stood next to the door ushering everyone out, I gave her a kiss and embraced her in a hug so affable and warm it could melt snow.

"I have been talking to grandma…" I whispered. She released from the hug and met my gaze.

"Oh honey, me too. Every night before I go to bed…in my prayers." She spoke. I just smiled and turned to leave as she reached out and gently grabbed my shoulder. "Give her all my love." She softly said.

"I will mom. I love you." I told her. What was I thinking, saying that to her? I guess I expected her to be experiencing the magic like I was. Maybe I just *wanted* her to. Then she could stop telling dad she was going to yoga when really, she was parking by the bridge, the one that Tillie and Enzi tried to force us in, and violently cries. What it must be like to lose your mom and dad and then have your own daughters try to kill you for some insurance money. I recognize the signs; they all point to clinical depression.

I arrived home at around half pass eight and walked up to the front door. as I wedged the key into the lock, a sensation from deep down in my gut began to fire warning messages through my body up to my brain, telling me not to open the door and not to go inside. I trusted the feeling and pulled the key out of the lock on the door and walked over to the trellis.

"Okay Grandma…" I said as I spoke to the morning glories, "…what are you trying to tell me?" I turned my head to the side and pressed my ear up to the biggest bloom. I keenly listened, but nothing was said. Instead I heard a voice, a startling but soft voice. I followed it out to the strawberry fields as it appeared to float on the air. I stood next to the fence post—the same one where grandma and I found grandpa—and noticed that there were a lot more lightning bugs than normal, an unbelievable amount. I stared at them, enthralled. They were so beautiful the way their intermittent flickers would light up the field, like a candle lit vigil, but something didn't feel right. "What am I missing?" I asked the breeze. Unexpectedly, the sky lit up. All the lightning bugs began to horde and light up, becoming a cloud of golden dust in the moon light more beautiful than anything I had ever laid eyes on, but I knew it was a warning. I watched as they appeared to file into a formation in the form of words, only two: *They're Inside.* I took a step back and focused once more on the emblazoned caution that looked like a marquee suspended in the sky as the words dissipated, and the majesty of the peaceful lightning bugs calmed the air once more. "They're inside…" I repeated to myself. "They're…" I thought, "…more than one?" I trusted the magic of the fields as I decided, instead of going inside and facing whatever was inside, to call the police instead.

"9-1-1, what is your emergency?" The operator asked.

"Yes, I believe I have intruders in my house. I live out on Maple Road, Maple Creek Farm…maybe you've heard of it?" I asked.

"Yes sir, I will send a unit right over…" She professionally said, "…do not attempt to go inside and thwart the intruders." I looked out over the field and thinned a smile.

"Thank you, grandma." I spoke.

I waited by the fence until I saw the dim glow of red and blue as they floated on the dust clouds. I walked over to the car as the police officer parked next to my car. Before I could even begin to explain why I thought there were intruders in my house, the front door burst open.

"What the fuck, Charles, you called the cops?" Raven shouted as she stormed over to where we were standing. Tillie and Enzi were cowering behind Raven, in her shadow. "It's okay, officer, I'm his wife." Raven said as she tried to link arms with me. I quickly pulled away, placing distance between us. I used to be able to recognize her, but not anymore, she had finally been corrupted.

"Sir, is this your wife?" The officer asked.

"Hell no! We've been divorced for almost a year." I began to explain. "And these two…" I said as I pointed at Tillie and Enzi. They had panic in their eyes and, when I looked at them, I saw them as they were when they were innocent children. "Look officer; I just want all of them gone. And I do not want to see them around here ever again." My hands were balled up into fists and shaking.

"Yes sir, come by in the morning and file for a restraining order." He said. The last time that I had dealt with this officer, I was donating money to one of their *Shop-with-a-cop* events, clearly, he remembered my generous donation. I thanked him for his assiduousness as he escorted Raven, Tillie and Enzi to his patrol car. Enzi stopped and turned to look at me.

"This is grandma and grandpas house; I have a right to be here!" She demanded.

"Grandma and Grandpa?" I asked. "The same people that the two of you tried to kill?" She rolled her eyes and scoffed.

"Oh, you'll never let that one go, will you?" She asked.

"No…" I replied stoically, "…and I bought the house. It's mine now." I haughtily but proudly told her as the officer told her to get into the cop car. The dull sound from the slamming of the car door sent shivers down my spine. I watched as they drove away, growing smaller and smaller in the distance until all that remained was the haze from the dust cloud, discharged by the police car tires.

"Thank you, grandma…" I said as I stopped by the trellis and pressed my face against the chilly leaves. "I know you wouldn't have warned me unless they had wicked intent." A breeze wafted by as it pushed a flower against my cheek.

"If you see a charmer, then nearby there is bound to be a snake." She whispered. I smiled, appreciatively.

"I understand now, thank you grandma." I said as I waited for a reply; but nothing was said. Just the rustle of leaves as they blew in the wind.

I tossed and turned all night like a small boat in a hurricane as I contemplated the happenings of earlier. "what were they doing here?" I asked myself. I knew mom would be here in the morning for coffee and I decided that I would tell her what happened and recommend to her and dad to change the locks at their house, and that I would even pay for it. I submitted the song about forgiveness to Ripp earlier and had finally gotten a response which calmed my mind and eased me to sleep. "Sensational! You have done it again!" I smiled and looked out the window as a glimmer of lightning bugs crawled on the outside of the panes, keeping watch over me. No doubt grandmas doing.

Chapter Five

I immediately awoke from a deep slumber due to a sensation of being suffocated as I sat up in bed. My chest was rising and falling as I calmed my pulse down from an alarming rate, I stared at the chair next to the window which was spotlighted by the full moon. Nobody was in the chair; it was completely empty. But *something* was in the chair, invisibly twirling a morning glory the way that I had done before. I stared as it danced back and forth between invisible fingertips.

"Grandma?" I watchfully spoke as I slowly reached for the lamp. As my fingers rested on the light switch, I observed that the flower had stopped spinning and just sat there suspended in the air. I flipped on the light switch and at that exact moment, the morning glory fell.

"So odd…" I thought to myself as I gazed—not blinking—at the flower. I let out a sigh and averted my gaze. "Grandma, you pick odd hours to make yourself known." I said, speaking to the flower.

I have so much built-up rage deep inside of me. It stems from the one thing that can age you faster than carcinogens, hate and regret. I hated Tillie and Enzi for what they did, and I regret not going behind mom and dad's back and reporting them to the authorities. I regret not giving grandma the attention she deserved, labeling her behavior as dementia instead of what it really was: magic.

I opened my eyes and was surprised to see that I was standing face to face with the morning glories. The chill of the early morning dew as it rested on the leaves, waiting to be evaporated by the sun.

"Hello…" I spoke as all the flowers opened their petals, one after the other, until they were all on display. My eyes widened as I counted every bloom; thirty-one.

"You will never get up that mountain with downhill thoughts." Grandma whispered through the vines. I sighed, irritatingly.

"Grandma, I'll admit that the conundrums keep me guessing, but can we just have a normal conversation? I am conflicted." I said as I slumped my shoulders forward. "Mom is depressed. I don't know what Tillie and Enzi are planning and Raven…she's too far gone." I said. The more I talked, getting everything off my chest and out there in the open, the better I felt. This must be why people feel better after visiting with a shrink.

"Do you feel better?" Grandma asked. I smiled through clenched teeth and blue lips. I did not realize that I was cold as I stood outside talking to the morning glories. *I'll just rest here*; grandpa must have thought when he felt this sting of cold.

"I had better get inside before I catch my death in a cold." I shivered. The flowers, one by one, closed their blooms becoming nothing more than cocoons, protected from the elements. I watched the biggest bloom as it turned to face me. "Oh yea, mom sends all of her love." I told the biggest bloom. It shook off all the dew that had collected on its petals and snapped shut with quickness.

I had just placed two logs on the fire and sprinkled some kindling to feed the soul of the fire which now roared and warmed the house. I had my hands wrapped around a fresh cup of coffee as I waited the first brag from the rooster, announcing the arrival of a new day.

"You will never get up that mountain with downhill thoughts." I said as I wrote those words over and over on my notepad, I knew what grandma was telling me. I was so afraid to fail that I refused to try, therefore failing. Most people fail due to lack of trying, those are the types of people I would rebuke in a song that I would write for someone else.

"I am such a hypocrite." I told myself. Here I am with all the tools for success, but I am failing due to lack of trying. "I need to change..." I proudly spoked as a wave of new energy rushed over me. The type of energy that tells you that you can do anything, that you are worth it and that you have a spark inside of you that is ready to ignite, all that is left is how you choose to light the match. Do you want to run with the bulls or hide behind the fence? "I'm going to run with the bulls, grandma." I triumphantly shouted as the apex of the sun peaked over the hills and painted the land with a new day, void from the happenings of yesterday. The rooster crowed, announcing the arrival of the sun, and acted as natures alarm clock, waking up the world...waking up *my* world.

Chapter Six

Forgiveness Train

Book your ticket, forgiveness train,

Please, oh please don't forsake this pain.

Book your ticket, forgiveness train,

Forgiveness train, forgiveness train.

If you hold onto the bad you will never get the good

You will never learn to trust, and you will be misunderstood.

Forgiveness is a train, and it can be unstoppable

It will help you look your age, and it will help you cleanse your soul.

A train that has no brakes is a metaphor for hate,

You can take it to the grave but it's never too late.

To forgive all those who have ever done you wrong

And your veins will pump a melody to your forgiveness song.

Book your ticket, forgiveness train,

Please, oh please don't forsake this pain.

Book your ticket, forgiveness train,

Forgiveness train, forgiveness train.

Jealousy, anger, hate and revenge will all just cause you wrinkles

Don't let it slow you down like you just fell into a sinkhole.

Instead just do a hair flip and then look the other way

You'll be happier when you stop listening to what they say.

You see this is what happens when you let anger win,

Your heart goes in a blender oh watch it watch it spin.

So do yourself a favor and just learn to forgive

So you can go through life and you can really start to live.

I turned on the television and flipped the channel over to MTV. They were chatting about an up-and-coming rising star, Ellipses was her name, and her number one hit *Forgiveness Train* was rising higher and higher to the number one spot on the Billboard Top 200. Ripp had sent a congratulatory bottle of champagne with a note: *You've done it again!* I turned off the television and stared at the note, in fine spirits. Sure, I had written songs for some of the industry's best, but never had one of my songs risen so fast to the top of the charts. I turned on the radio just as the radio host began his announcement.

"Up next, ELLIPSES, and her number one hit: Forgiveness Train." I sat there smiling even bigger than before, my eyes closed as I immersed myself in every single word. Ellipses loved my song so much so, that she didn't change one word. Maybe this was my chance to start singing my own songs. I had already proven myself worthy as a successful song writer, maybe it *was* time for me to reach new objectives, to reach new heights. Grandma once told me that if you're not working towards your next goal, then you are satisfied with being mediocre.

I opened the window and pulled back the curtains, "Grandma, listen to this song, I wrote it after you inspired me." I joyfully stated as I stood up and swayed back and forth to the beat of the song. "This is because of you, grandma." I sang to her. I stood there next to the window, dancing, hoping that grandma could hear the song, hoping that she could hear the words.

"And what is going on here?" A soft voice asked, bringing me down from my high. I turned around, winded like a dog in the heat, and saw mom.

"Hey mom!" I shouted as the music blared over the speakers, "…you hear this song?" She sauntered over to the speaker and turned down the volume.

"Honey, everyone can hear the song." She said. I was about to say something as she held up her hand. "Ripp sent it over to me this morning. I've listened to it like seven times. Honey, I am so proud of you." She said, enveloping me in a hug. I smiled and embraced the hug. Grandma used to tell me that no two hugs are the same, and I always believed that they were all different, like hand lines or fingerprints, but moms hugs always felt like grandmas' hugs: different but the same.

"Mom, do you believe in magic?" I asked, fickly and preparing to choose my next words warily. I studied her facial movements and her body language as she walked over to the window, putting her hand on the windowsill—the paint cracking underneath her palms and chipping away—the slight crunch of the lead paint made me cringe and made my lip quiver slightly.

"Honey, the world is full of magic…" She began to say as she paused. A gentle wind blew through the window—through her hair—as she closed her eyes and inhaled deeply. "Mmmm, strawberry fields." She said. "This is a very familiar smell; I think she is happy." I looked at her with a smug look and one eyebrow lifted.

"Who?" I asked, the breeze dancing around the room like a wind tango.

"What are you, an owl?" She asked. I laughed and joined her at the window. I looked her in the eyes and slowly separated my lips.

"Whoo…whooo…" I hooted as I attempted to mimic an owl. "Come here…I want to show you something." I said as I led her outside to the trellis of morning glories. "Say hi…" I said as I pointed to the stunning assortment of morning glories, so vivacious and pulsating with the colors of blue lavender, purple and fuchsia.

"It won't work." She said as she reached down and grabbed my hand, studying the wall of flowers. I looked at her, eyes life-sized and sodden like a child who can't comprehend why their dog ran away. "Charles, if this is how you talk to grandma, you need to keep it between you two." I stood there, confused and upset. This was her mother, and she didn't want to talk to her? Nothing seemed to make sense anymore.

"Which way is up, mom?" I asked.

"It is whichever way your heart leads you." She said, philosophically. "I talk to grandma in my own magical way." Somehow what she said, her words so soft—like velvet—calmed my nerves. I finally understood then and there what was said to me all those years ago. *If you happen to stumble upon a bit of magic, don't ask questions.* My posture relaxed, becoming less taut and unyielding.

"Coffee?" I asked.

I pulled the warm croissants out of the oven—so golden and fluffy—and spread some cinnamon butter on them. We imbibed as the smells of freshly baked croissants, coffee and strawberry fields permeated our senses.

"So, honey, why didn't you tell the officer about what Tillie and Enzi did?" Mom asked as the steam rose off her coffee, dancing around the air.

"I was going to…" I began to say as I paused to wash down the crumbs that lingered in my mouth. "But when I looked at them with their eyes so full of fear, I saw them as they were when they were innocent little girls…scared of the monsters in the closet."

"Do you remember when you and Trevor took turns sleeping in shifts in their closet?" She asked as she sighed. "…I miss them being that age." I wanted to smile for her, but I just couldn't bring myself to. I tried not to show on my face that sleeping in their closet—protecting them—was one of my most cherished memories. But it has since vanished, now being inundated by the look on Enzi's face that day at the bridge as she gritted her teeth and wrapped her fingers so tightly around the steering wheel that they turned pallid. And the possessed look in Tillie's eyes as her smile widened the closer we got to the edge of the wall on the bridge, like they could taste and feel the insurance money.

"Well, mom, now they have become the very monsters that were in their closet." I callously said.

"Maybe…" mom began to say, "…but a great man I once knew said that if you hold onto the bad you will never get the good." She smiled, warming my frozen heart.

"You really did listen to the song?" I asked as she laced her fingers through mine, so warm and soft.

"I always do, sweetie. I always do."

Chapter Seven

It had been five arduous months of sitting in a cramped recording studio that smelled like wet cardboard after a rainstorm. It took a bit of convincing for my label to sign me as a singer/songwriter instead of just a songwriter, but once they did, the work began. I had offered to pay for my own studio time if they paid the music producer and sound mixers and they agreed. I recorded my first single, *Shine*, and they released it just to see where I would fall in the rankings. To my surprise, it landed right on the Billboard charts. My first album was set to launch exactly three months from now and I still had five more songs to record, I was exhausted, and I was uncertain, but I absolutely loved what I was doing.

"How is my shining star?" Ripp asked as he walked into the recording studio where I had been for nearly twelve hours. He looked at me as I appeared emaciated and plain worn out. "Give me a moment with him guys…" Ripp said to the sound engineers as everyone left the booth. He motioned for me to come out of the booth and sit with him.

"Hey Ripp, what's up?" I asked.

"You tell me, what's going through your mind?" He asked as he visibly inspected me. "You look like shit." I smiled a little.

"Thanks…I think…" I said as I sighed. "…I haven't spoken to grandma in a few months. It's like the moment she put it in my mind to push myself further, to sing my *own* songs, she left me…" I told him. He studied me further with a mystified look on his face.

"Are we talking about a different grandparent? Didn't she die?" He asked, disconcerted. "I mean, have you been sleeping?" He looked at me like I was crazy and maybe having a nervous breakdown. "Look, just focus on the now. Let's get this album finished and then we can worry about other things." He said.

"Spoken like a true manager…" I sarcastically said.

"You're right, that was insensitive. Maybe try to talk to her from a different approach." He suggested. I was so consumed with recording that I hadn't even thought about that.

"That is actually a really good idea, thank you." I told him as he smiled and nodded, almost agreeing with himself. "You're right; I need to focus on the songs and the album." I said.

"Okay, I'll go get the sound mixers and the producer. Make me proud!" He said as he left, and I got back into the booth.

I got home that night as the watch on my wrist beeped, I looked down and smiled: 11:11 PM. "Make a wish." I said to myself as I looked up at the night sky. It was so pitch black and dappled with a dazzling array of stars in every direction. The occasional wisp of vanilla clouds hovering silently, and a tender draft mixed it all together to create a perfect memory. I had been working so many hours over the last five months that I had forgotten to slow down and enjoy the little things, the free things. I closed my eyes and inhaled deeply just to take it all in. this was the first time in months that I had felt free from the restraints of wet cardboard that tainted the inside of my nose: I could breathe again. I thought about what I wanted to wish for, I could literally wish for anything: money, fame, fortune, a Lamborghini, and a cheetah named Chester. But none of that enticed me. It wasn't what I wanted. I opened my eyes and traced the tail of a shooting star as it traveled from one side of the sky to the other. "I wish…" I began to say softly before I stopped, gathering my wish. "I wish that mom finds happiness." I said as I kissed my thumb and pressed it up against the night sky.

I locked the car and walked up the winding path to the front door. As I got to the front door, I placed the key in the lock and then paused, pulling it out. "What the hell." I said as I turned and walked over to the trellis and the barrage of morning glories. I stuck my hand inside the bush, feeling a handful of vines that wrapped around each other as the coldness of the stems made me feel at ease.

"Grandma, are you there?" I softly asked. I looked up and counted the blooms as I waited for a response: thirty-three. The last time I had counted, there were thirty-one. "Hmm, two more…" I said to myself. I wondered if there was some type of a connection between grandma talking to me and new blooms of morning glories. Then I thought back to what grandma told me all those years ago: *If you stumble upon a bit of magic, don't ask questions.* I sat there for another fifteen minutes as the temperature began to drop more and more. "I know I haven't been the best person lately, grandma, and I apologize. I am here when you are ready to talk. I love you." I said as I leaned forward to kiss the closest morning glory, but it snapped shut. Maybe it wasn't the fields that I smelled but it was a strand of resentment that was overpowering the wet cardboard that lived in my nasal cavity.

I walked inside and put a log on the fire and then knelt, watching the flames dance. The colors of the flames always gave me reprieve; they always reminded me too how to be humble. I haven't built a fire since I started recording my songs. I poked the fire with the cast iron fire poker and got up off my knee and sat in the chair, just watching the fire dance around in swirls. The green flame was always my favorite; it always reminded me of greed being put in its place. Of remembering where we come from and always being grateful for what you have and what you don't have.

I didn't receive a message from grandma that night, but then again, I think I did. She silently told me what I had been running from for the last five months, myself. I had forgotten where I came from as I fell into the dark, sinister side of my heart. The dark side doesn't appreciate things, is ungrateful and mean. Sometimes when you have lived on the dark side for too long, like Raven, Tillie, and Enzi, it's nearly impossible to come back to the light side. I realized this and was so thankful to have caught myself before it was too late. I needed to find a happy medium where I could sing my songs, work hard, create and still be my old, humble self. I didn't want to end up like other artists who get so consumed with fame and fortune that they forget where they come from. I knew the morning glories were still mad at me, but over time I figured they would see the steps I was taking to right my wrongs and they would eventually forgive me.

Chapter Eight

I followed the same mundane routine that I had grown accustomed to over the last few months: wake up; brush my teeth whilst showering; get dressed while chanting my mantra: *I can do anything I put my mind to*, drink my coffee and leave for the studio.

"Good morning grandma." I said to the morning glories as I walked pass them, clutching my coffee and my notebook. On this day—as the sun was burning off the morning haze that hung low—the wind blew a message pass my ears.

"Poodle, be in love, you'll be happy." I stopped in my tracks, dropped my coffee and my notebook and ran back to the trellis of morning glories, thirty-four in total, all fully bloomed and trumpeting as a hummingbird buzzed merrily along from bloom-to-bloom nourishing in sweet, sweet nectar.

"Grandma…are you there?" I anxiously asked. I was stirring the tears as they welled up in my eyes.

"Of course, I am here, Poodle." She said as I finally opened the valve to my emotions and released the pressure which had built up over the course of five months. I was sobbing (manly sobs, of course) as I fell to my knees. "There, there Poodle, the weatherman didn't predict rain today." She said as I detected a cackle that floated on a puff of air. Even in death or in the Ever After, wherever she currently was, she still had her sardonic sense of humor.

"I'm sorry for how I have been acting grandma." I said as I slowed my breathing and calmed myself down. "I took your advice and started singing my own songs, they really like me grandma." I tried my hardest to resonate myself as meek and affable.

"From what your mother tells me, they love you." She said softly. I walked back to my notebook and picked it up, dusting off the remnants of the Earth: soil and grass. I sat cross legged on the ground in front of the trellis as a morning glory, broken at the stem, sat on the cold ground next to me. I thumbed through the pages of my notebook which, as of late, were full of scribbles: libretto, verse, poems, and ideas. It was a peak into the deepest chasm of my soul. I read to her the lyrics from *Forgiveness Train*. "I remember this song; I was there, in the room, when you wrote it silly." She said.

"Is that where you have been the last five months, with mom? Are you still mad at me?" I supplicated. I still needed resolution to the emptiness which inhabited my heart. The moment grandma's voice floated pass my ears this morning; she acted as the landlord to my heart and evicted the emptiness without delay.

"Well honey, I was with your mother and I was never mad at you. Even I can't be in two places at once. I'm still figuring this entire thing out. She just needed me more than you did." She said as I sighed in relief. I thought back to about a week ago when I looked up at the indigo-stained night sky, speckled with twinkling stars, and made a wish. I wished for mom to be happy, on the tail end of a shooting star, I guess it came true. This was fixing to be a *particularly good* day.

"Grandma, I have to get to the studio. I am finishing the last two songs for the album; I will be back. I love you." I said as I hesitated to leave. I stood there, smiling, as I reached up to touch a big bloom that faced the sun. it quickly snapped shut as my finger grazed the brim of the petal, startling me.

"I thought you were leaving?" Grandma joked. I chuckled back as I sensed her question was more of a rhetorical one.

"Will you be here when I get back?" I asked. It was a fair question, I thought to myself. I had just gotten her back after all these months, and what's better, she wasn't mad at me. She was with someone who needed her more than I did.

"I will be here as long as I am not needed elsewhere. But remember, be in love, you'll be happy." She said. And just like that, all thirty-four of the morning glories turned to soak up the warmth of the sun as they released a sweet fragrance that no scientists could bottle, not even if they tried. The cheerful buzzing of the bees as they pollinated from one bloom to another and the happy flit of hummingbirds as they zoomed back and forth put to rest any darkness that loomed inside of me. I was finally me again; I was the old Charles that everyone loved.

I walked into the studio with a much sunnier disposition, like I had grandma floating close by guiding me. The sound engineers, as of late, had even gone so far as to evade any of the formalities which are instilled in all of us as children in the form of manners, I was gradually becoming the hollow artist that they loathed working with.

"Good morning everyone, I brought coffee and doughnuts." I said happily as I greeted each one of them. "Listen everyone, I would like to apologize for my abhorrent behavior. Lately I have been going through some things…" I explained as I paused. "…It's not important what, but I am back. Baby I am back!" I shouted as I propelled my fist into the air. "This is going to be a great day!" They all looked at each other, perplexed, but receptive as they accepted my apology and enjoyed the coffee and doughnuts. "Okay gentlemen, ready to make a hit?" I asked. With that, I went into recording booth with a new scuttle of verve, like how it must feel after a hurricane strikes and you get back to find that your house was the only one to survive, unscathed.

We worked obstinately, making sure that everything was faultless. I ordered pizza for the booth and everyone sat around savoring the smells of parmesan, marinara sauce and pepperoni and shared horror stories about past singers who were awful to work with. I happily joined in conversation, only being compared to other artists as the "eighth worse on a scale from one to ten", but because I thoughtfully apologize *and* bought pizza, they were happy to increase my ranking from eight to ten.

"I am happy with that." I joked. I sat there, looking around the room and contemplated, silently, as everyone was playing on their phones, scrolling through Twitter, Facebook, and Instagram. I closed my eyes and inhaled deeply, expecting to breathe in an overwhelming scent of Italy. But no, the sweet scent of morning glories was permeating throughout the booth and the sound mixing room. "Hmm…" I said, inhaling.

"Is everything okay Mr. Charles?" A man—Dave—asked as he studied me.

"It doesn't smell like we cardboard anymore." I said. He looked around as everyone was engaged in banter with one another and inhaled for himself.

"You're right. It smells sweet, what is that?" He asked as he looked around, expecting to see a can of Febreze or some type of air freshener hanging nearby.

"It is the smell of morning glories." I said as I Looked at him with a sliver of a smile. "I brought it from home." He smiled back, inhaled deeply one more time and let out a perceptible exhale.

"Well I like it, please bring it back!" He said. I looked around happily and smiled, squinting my eyes slightly under the fluorescent lights.

"I like it too…" I began to say out loud to myself, "…I like it too."

Chapter Nine

The air was marked, tainted with mendacity and treachery which was perfectly hidden behind broad smiles with red stained lips and glowing white teeth.

We all sat around the back patio underneath the loggia at grandma and grandpas festively talking and enjoying the many gifts that we had been adorned with in the form of blessings. Blessings to have both of your grandparents still alive at this age and able to enjoy a day such as this. Tillie and Enzi were not so much talking as they were intently listening. Mom had just announced, loosely, that she and dad increased their life insurance policy from five-hundred thousand to seven hundred fifty thousand dollars.

"Enough to make sure you kids are well taken care of after we pass." Mom said as she smiled and looked around. I perceptibly watched the sky as it unexpectedly distorted from a beautiful azure to a deceitful gray. I could feel the tension in the barometric pressure of the atmosphere as the conversations between everyone else went on as if a sudden change in the weather didn't just abruptly shift.

"Was I the only one who could see or sense the change?" I thought to myself as I looked around and just watched everyone as they were all engaged in banter with one another…well almost everyone. Grandma had pulled her chair in front of the morning glories and just sat there harmlessly talking to the flowers while Tillie and Enzi were in their own little world at the other end of the patio.

"Enzi, did you hear what mom and dad said?" Tillie asked as she leaned close to Enzi, whisper distance.

"Yeah. Would be nice if that happened sooner rather than later." Enzi uncaringly stated.

Her thoughts as of late where dripping with cruelty and gloom. I fear it had something to do with the religion—cult—that they joined. *The Mystic Mile*, started by a skinny woman with hair the color of yellow hay and a hollow from collar bone to collar bone, so small and concaved it could be considered a pirate's dream in the form of a sunken chest. It's as if she had been kicked square in the chest with the force of one thousand donkeys. And her eyes, once sparkling and green were now sallow, barely visible through the bags under her eyes which were no doubt brought on by drugs and lack of sleep.

Enid Rasp is her name. She had discovered The Mystic Mile while she was serving twenty years for extortion and aggravated assault, but due to a technicality they regrettably had to release her. She went off the grid for a few years as she built up her fan base and now, she resides with Tillie and Enzi. Everyone stressed our concerns about Enid Rasp, but we were quickly shot down.

"Don't judge a book by its cover!" They would say. But the thing is that this book had no cover, impossible to read in the most precarious of ways.

"I'm going to call Enid Rasp right now and tell her that I think I found a possible "donor" for The Mystic Mile." Enzi said to Tillie as she was nearly overcome with excitement.

I leaned in towards mom as she mirrored my movements. "Everything okay, honey?" She asked as I anxiously watched Tillie get up and go stand by grandma next to the morning glories.

"I think the girls are up to something mom. Something is not right." I quietly said. She looked at me and signed.

"I'm sure it's nothing honey." I sighed and let her go back to her conversation with dad and grandpa as she reached back over and held grandpa's hand. He gave it a slight squeeze, appreciatively. I got up and walked over to where grandma was sitting just as Tillie began speaking to grandma.

"Hey grandma…" Tillie began to say as she ran her fingers through grandma's hair, roughly. "…When you die, can I pawn all of your jewelry?" She coldly asked as she grasped a clump of hair and yanked it hard.

"OUCH!" Grandma shouted. I hurried over to grandma's aid, filled to the brim with ire, and pushed Tillie so hard that her heel broke and she fell backwards and scraped her wrist.

"Charles, what the FUCK was that for?" She screamed as everyone rushed over to see what the commotion was.

"Charles…" Mom austerely began to scold as grandma, sardonic as ever, turned to look at Tillie.

"Next time don't pull my hair…and no, you can't have my jewelry. It will go to the morning glories!" I looked at mom, darting my eyes back and forth from grandma to dad and then over to grandpa. Everyone seemed to have vexed energy hanging over their heads like a storm cloud.

"Still think it's nothing mom?" I asked, ascetically. She snapped as she caught my eyes with her motherly gaze. The kind that says *Don't push me, boy.*

"Hush, Charles." She said as she looked around at everyone as the disposition seemed to change and everyone, except for Tillie and Enzi, had circled up around grandma. "It's almost time for our reservation…" Mom began to say as she pointed directly at Tillie, "…you and Enzi will be there. This is a family dinner!" I looked at Tillie, eyes filled with discontent, as she shot me a look back that said *No one believes you.*

"I think you are confused, grandma…" Tillie softly but cruelly said as Enzi walked up to where we were all standing, putting her phone in her back-right pocket. "…But I accept your apology." She arrogantly said. Grandma began to hysterically laugh as she pointed at the biggest bloom of the morning glories.

"We didn't apologize. Everything that is sweet eventually turns sour, you rotten, rotten fruit." She shifted her gaze from the morning glories over to where Tillie and Enzi were standing and pointed her delicate, trembling finger at them. I helped grandma up from the chair and linked arms with her, escorting her to my SUV.

"I'll drive mom…" I hollered. "Why don't you, dad and grandpa ride with me?" Mom smiled and closed her door.

"Okay dear."

Tillie and Enzi followed behind us in Enzi's vehicle—a full size truck that was entirely too big for her.

"So, what did Enid Rasp say?" Tillie asked. Enzi smiled diabolically and looked at her through unrecognizable eyes.

"We take care of them tonight." Enzi said as she tightened her grip around the steering wheel as if it were a brittle neck.

"Tonight?!" Tillie responded, stunned. "That doesn't leave much room for planning or error!" Enzi laughed once more as she looked over at Tillie.

"We will ram their vehicle on the bridge and push them into the river. But after dinner, we may as well enjoy one last supper with everyone." Enzi coldly said. Tillie threw her head back and laughed as the weary sun glistened off her hair and her coffee-stained skin.

"That is so twisted!" She said as they pulled into the restaurant parking lot. They looked at each other, pushed the release button on the seat belts and, as it snapped back, they chanted *GAME TIME!*

As we walked into the restaurant, grandma and I tailed behind the others as we walked at a slower pace. Grandma squeezed my arm and stopped walking.

"Grandma, are you okay?" I asked. She had a look of concern unlike any I had ever. She reached her arms up and cupped her hands around my face, pulling me in for a kiss on each cheek.

"Don't leave me, Poodle. Don't let those rotten fruit be alone with me." I looked at her eyes and could see that she didn't have much fight left. Her tired eye lids struggled to stay all the way open as her lips quivered. "Promise me."

"I promise, grandma. I will not take my eyes off you." I said as she smiled and slapped me in the center of the back.

"Well then, let's go!" She joyfully said. I smiled as we linked arms and strode into the restaurant.

Chapter Ten

The sky had just lowered its gauze-like veil—like that of a bride before the groom lifts it up and over, revealing a new day awash with memories of future past. The windshield, blurred by the pitter patter of swollen raindrops, sang a song in Morse code on the windshield.

"Angel tears…" Grandma used to tell me, "…someone with a heart so pure just took their last breath."

Dinner was gauche to say the least. Not because Tillie and Enzi were wicked and plotting to kill their loved ones for insurance money. No, awkward because they were enjoying this last supper, the way a cat injures a mouse and then plays with it—sweet torture. *Please don't take my dignity*, the mouse must be squeaking as the cat bats him from paw to paw.

Grandma never took her hand from mine as she ate and drank with her other hand. Eyes valiant like a hawk that has just spotted its prey, she never took her eyes off Tillie and Enzi. And I never took my eyes off her. You see, grandma liked everybody and did not have trust issues, so why now? Why these two? She trusted in the universe, the wind, the trees and even in the morning glories.

"The wind hears all, Poodle." She once told me as I pondered what she could possibly mean. But it meant everything *and* nothing all at the same time; the wind is both everywhere and nowhere all at once.

"I have to use the latrine." Grandpa announced. That was always his sly way of paying the check before everyone else could play Russian roulette with credit cards.

"Well, don't fall in this time." Grandma quickly fired back as she laughed. Spaghetti sauce danced around her face with every bite.

"Here grandma, let me help you." I said as she brushed off my words.

"Don't bother; I'll just keep making more of a mess. It's spaghetti, after all." She happily said as she twirled more noodles onto the tines of her fork.

Sean, Trevor, and their families left the restaurant first; it was a school night after all. Mom, dad, and grandpa hugged and kissed Tillie and Enzi—overwhelmed that the hug option was in the cards. Mom seemed quite apprehensive—the hug—was so bitter and compulsory, but she exuded so much radiant energy that it hijacked their bitter hug and made it warm. Warm like that time we took a family boat trip to the lake—so shiny and sparkling with the ripples of the sun.

"Faster daddy, faster…" Trevor and I would bellow through energized breaths. Tillie and Enzi gripped their popsicles and nothing else. The boat propelled forward with such force that Tillie and Enzi went flying off the back of the boat like the concussion from a grenade, bobbing up and down in the water like apples in a barrel. When they were finally retrieved—cradled in mom and dad's arms—for the first time in their lives they truly felt love and safety in the form of heat and warmth from a loved one's touch.

"Okay…" Enzi began to say. "…We watch them drive away and then we tail them." Tillie, still feeling the effects from the hug, slightly hesitated.

"What about Charles?" She asked.

"Collateral damage." Enzi said. "With him gone, the money will get split four ways instead of five, which means we get more!" She greedily stated as she reached down and shifted the lever into 4-HI.

"Are we sure about this?" Tillie asked. Enzi looked at her sharply, unrecognizable.

"Do you want to reach a state of enlightenment or not?" Enzi asked. Tillie—a puppy with her tail between her legs—bit her tongue and submitted.

"Of course, I do…" She said as Enzi nodded to her.

I shut my car door and looked around to make sure that everyone had their seat belts on.

"Ooh, Poodle, take the bridge." Grandma excitedly suggested, spaghetti sauce now dried in patches around her face.

"Okay, grandma." I said as she happily clapped her hands and beamed a smile.

As we got to the bridge—a single lane with hip high stone walls—grandma's eyes lit up. She always had a strong respect for bridges. The river had become swollen, as if it had been stung by a hornet's nest. Suddenly, the sound of crunching metal and a thunderous boom clapped as our heads whipped back in our seats. We had just been rammed. As I Flung my head around, all I could see were two intensely bright lights, acerbic and cruel, a hornet's nest to my aversion. It's as if time slowed to a crawl as the truck reversed and then rammed us again and again and again, inching us closer and closer to the edge of the river, closer to the stone wall. Dad shouted in shock.

"It's Tillie and Enzi!" Mom looked back in dismay, panic shining in her eyes like that of a Jewish mother being separated from her children as they were led to the gas chamber and she was led to the camps. Grandpa wrapped his arms around grandma and then dad wrapped his arms around them both, shielding them from possible debris from the next anticipated hit that was so certain to come.

"Charles…" Mom shouted as I Mashed my foot on the brake pedal.

"I know what to do…everyone hold on!" I shouted as I watched them reverse once more. We were just a few feet away from the wall—stones so cold and clad in moss—as I turned the wheels in the opposite direction and waited for their next strike. We waited for them to push us closer to the edge of the swollen river, which seemed to roar in anticipation of our unexpected arrival.

"Hit them again…HARDER!" Tillie shouted as her adrenaline spiked. It was almost like she had just gotten injected with an epinephrine shot.

"Shut up, Tillie!" Enzi shouted back as she expressed the same amount of exhilaration and energy. "Let's end this!" She frenziedly as she pressed the gas pedal all the way to the floor, screaming the tires and ripping up the earth as she slammed into the trunk of my SUV. My plan had worked as I pressed on the gas pedal upon impact. The pushed us in the direction of my wheels as we side swiped the cold stone wall and were free to hurriedly cross the bridge. We got on solid land as I parked nearly one hundred yards away from the river and checked on the well-being of everyone.

Mom was crying. Grandpa was visibly shaken but otherwise find and grandma just kept on babbling, lucidly.

"Rotten fruit…sour little rotten fruit!" I looked at dad, resentment sweltering in his eyes.

"I'm getting a gun." He said. Mom had always objected to dad's allure with hunting and guns, but upon her silence of dad's confession, I knew she would not fight him on this.

Enzi and Tillie remained parked in the middle of the bridge as big, sodden drops of rain—the sadness from the skies—caused smoke to billow from the radiator which had been pushed back into the engine and sprayed liquid emeralds all over the balloon-white hood of the truck.

"Enzi…" Tillie spoke, shaking like a leaf that is barely holding onto the changes of fall.

"Don't you say a fucking word, Tillie!" Enzi boorishly said. "Just play it cool." She put the vehicle in drive and activated the windshield wipers as they scraped the tears off the clear pane that severed them from the world. "Just laugh and act innocent." She said as they slowly drove up to where we were parked, trembling with our doors ajar.

"WHAT IN THE FU—" Dad began to bawl as they slowed their truck to a creep.

"Daddy, we were just playing around. April Fools!" Enzi festively said. I looked down at my watch, the date mocked me: April 1st. They drove off before any of us could say anything else, their truck sputtering and presenting smoke signals that could be seen for miles.

"Mom, we have to call the cops and report them. They can't get away with this." I pleaded as she studied my eyes like a pop quiz.

"Honey they will be arrested and charged with attempted murder. We can't let your two sisters go to jail; people die in jail." Mom said as I held up my hands, mouth agape in awe. "Besides, maybe this was just a harmless April Fool's Day joke gone horribly wrong."

"Why are you protecting them?" I yelled as my hands balled up into small fists. "They could have killed us all. We're all just lucky that I took that defensive driving course." I was now the one with adrenaline running through my veins. I knew this wasn't the time or the place for this argument as I lowered my voice, not wanting to scare grandma any more than she might be.

"Well that was a fun ride, who wants to get back in line?" Grandma joked. I looked at mom and then caught eyes with dad and grandpa as we all broke into fits of laughter. Grandma found her audience and kept the jokes coming. "Next time, I want to ride in *their* vehicle."

I love grandma; even amid misguided demise, she tried to alter the mood with her ironic humor and quick wit. "Charles threw up his dinner…" She said as she pointed to grandpa. "Let's get more spaghetti."

"Let's go…" I suggested as we all piled back into the SUV. I drove everyone back to grandma and grandpa's house, hoping—begging— that Tillie and Enzi weren't there. "Mom, we *will* talk about this later." I said as she waved her unstable hand, dismissing my lexis completely.

Chapter Eleven

In a world ruled by propinquity, time is a valued commodity that no one seems to possess. I learned this in the hardest of ways as I found grandma lying on her back in an eternal slumber without breath in a pile of dead morning glories; black as ash they were, like they had been charred.

"Charles, tell me how you feel." Mom said as she consoled my weeping core.

"It feels like I just completed a fifteen-thousand-piece puzzle only to find that I was missing the last piece upon completion." I told her.

That old eclectic lamp, the one with the light purple lamp shade, reminiscent of memories from the past—a hair barrette clipped to Enzi's pigtails when she was seven—and the vase that held all of grandma's treasures. Grandma had grown attached to her daily adventures with the lamp and *always* placed her most prized treasure; an *I Love Lucy* pendant that forever held Lucille Ball's face in mother-of-pearl inlay, became her lifeline.

Towards the end, grandma had a curious habit of unplugging anything and everything from all the outlets, including her favorite lamp. So on that night, that dreadful hour of darkness where twilight zephyrs refrigerate the tepid air and the smell of warm milk and freshly baked apple pie infiltrated the firmament, I put grandma to bed like I had done so many nights before—with her oxygen tube secured behind her ears as it hissed slightly, breathing time into her lungs. As she slept soundly, I plugged everything back into the walls and cleaned up the house—taking treasures from the lamp and trouncing them throughout the house once more.

But when my foot looped around the electrical cord form her favorite lamp, I took a step away as I pulled it to the ground and shattered it into one hundred and twenty-three pieces, yes, I counted. I hurried back into the room to check on grandma. I expected to find her sitting there in the shadows with her feeble legs dangling over the side of the bed—not quite touching the floor—and her hair a tousled mess. No, instead I found her oxygen tube lying on the floor, hissing like a mistrustful snake. She was gray and cold—like the stone wall from the bridge that was covered in moss—and she was covered in morning glories that were lifeless, the color of ash.

I alerted nobody at first as I sat with her, serenely, brushing her hair. I didn't cry just as she knew I wouldn't. Instead I celebrated her arrival to the Ever After, to be with grandpa and the morning glories—to be a morning glory. I called mom at midnight.

"I need you here now." Was all that I said as I hung up the phone and walked back into grandma's room and sat next to her on the bed with my hand in her hand, memorizing every detail of her face before she too became nothing more than the color of the morning glories: ash. I gazed at the window—the same window that grandma and I used to sit by as we would watch these two small red birds that nested at the top of the tree attack the crows that would try to steal their eggs—as a horde of lightning bugs looked in, weeping. The hum of anguished lightning bugs is too awful for words, and it changes from person to person, but to me it was the sound of the brakes on a train on a snowy cold track. The way they mourn is a spectacle of its own. Grandma must have meant a great deal to them for me to be able to hear their sad songs, so I did what anyone in my situation would have done.

"Why don't you come in?" I sympathetically suggested as I opened the window. One by one they crawled inside, their lights eternally on, illuminating the room and bringing light and color to grandma once more.

"What is going on here?" Mom suddenly asked as she stood at the doorway looking in. Her hand traced the wood grain on the mahogany door that grandpa carved for grandma when they got married, as a gift. Grandma was lustrous and once ashen morning glories had been given life and turned into bright hues of midnight purple, the color of happiness and bereavement.

"They're saying their goodbyes." I whispered to mom as she smiled and rested her head on my shoulder. We stood there, listening to the symphony of lightning bugs as their euphoric cries became a piece of music to our hearts. Time of death: 11:11 PM.

Chapter Twelve

Grandma once told me that in the Garden of Good and Evil, we are judged and then divided into good flowers and bad weeds. Those good flowers go on to do great things and change the world: Princess Diana, Joan of Arc, Ellen DeGeneres, Clay Aiken, Oprah, and Mother Theresa, to name a few. But for those in the Garden of Weeds: Norman Bates, the Unabomber, TSA Agents, Charles Manson, that evil kid from the movie The Butterfly Effect and all clowns (am I right?), they go on to wreak havoc. Enid Rasp, born with someone else's soul and evil eyes, well, she came from the Garden of Weeds.

When Enid Rasp was just a small child—seven to be exact— she set her first cat on fire. A tired old, gray street cat with one eye and the other one blanketed with fog. All this cat wanted was some compassion for the rest of his days. *Dare to dream, One Eye, dare to dream.* Instead, he met his end as he was lured inside the garage with bacon and then trapped inside of a doll house, doused in lighter fluid. The windows were too small to climb out of and all One Eye could do was helplessly watch as the glow from the match grew closer and closer as he watched helplessly through the small windows. The screams from One Eye as he frantically looked for a way out were awful. He was trapped, burning alive. Still to this day, One Eye's screams of agony and suffering haunt Enid Rasp in her darkest of nightmares.

When Enid Rasp was thirteen years old, she met a girl with hair as black as night. This girl call Enid names and poked fun at her. So, Enid took her teacher's scissors and cut off the girls' ponytail. Then, she braided that ponytail into hers, streaking raven black with brilliant blonde, as a trophy. She wore that striped ponytail proudly as the girl—discouraged—wore a beanie cap until the sting wore off. She never teased another person again.

Maybe if Enid Rasp were loved, hugged, and kissed more as a child, she would have had a fight chance. Maybe then, she wouldn't have grown into a product of hate, rage, fury, and suspicion.

When Enid Rasp was fourteen years old, she got her first taste of blood in the form of revenge. She ran away from home. *Off to some place less tragic than here*, she must have thought to herself as she climbed up into that eighteen-wheeler, bound for Nebraska. It took her one full week to trust the driver of the eighteen-wheeler, but only three minutes to lose her trust in him and in everything else.

She awoke suddenly as the driver had her pinned down. He was carving strange markings into the flesh of her abdomen; the way petroglyphs are carved into the sandstone walls of Arizona. The possessed look in his arctic, haunted eyes comforted her as she screamed.

"Deeper! Cut me Deeper!" He reached enlightenment through The Mystic Mile that night and Enid Rasp wanted what he had. So later that night, as he soundly slept. His invisible trophy of enlightenment hovered slightly above his head where only he could see it. Enid Rasp bashed in his skull with a tire iron. Too young to be tried as an adult, she became a product of the state, institutionalized. She discovered a family through The Mystic Mile and found love for the first time in her life.

Enzi and Tillie—who had struggled for years to find their tribe—accidentally came across a forum on the internet titled: *Something Better*.

"Is this what we are looking for?" Tillie asked, motioning for Enzi to peer at the computer screen. Enzi pushed her glasses up onto the bridge of her nose—the way they do in academia—and gloated as if she had found it instead of her.

"This is *exactly* what we're looking for!" She triumphed.

Months went by as they began to study the material, pay their monetary dues—that mom and dad unknowingly paid—and learned all they could about The Mystic Mile.

On their first mission from above, they were instructed to do something so horrific and macabre that it still haunts them; drown a kitten in a bucket of water and record it. Their first act of evil— which they did and compulsively fell in love with, just as Enid Rasp did—permitted them to join The Mystic Mile.

On the day that Enid Rasp moved in with Tillie and Enzi, they drove over to grandpa and grandma's house to get an extra bed frame and dining table, and everyone got to meet her.

"Oh, who is this?" Grandma asked as she grabbed Enid Rasp's hand.

"What's it to ya' old lady?" Enid Rasp offensively responded. Grandma studied her for a moment, sensing the malevolence, which was coursing through her veins, and began to enlighten her.

"If you can take ownership of your stories of struggle, then you can write your own ending." Grandma said as she let go of Enid Rasp's hand.

"What the hell does that mean lady…you are crazy!" She said as her mean, wounding words clipped the edges of her crooked teeth as she sprayed her lexis in grandma's vicinity. Grandma courteously smiled and ignored her as they took their leave without saying so much as a *thank you* or a *goodbye*.

Tillie and Enzi were added to a family thread in a group chat on our phones and everyone—me included—stressed our apprehension about Enid Rasp.

"Don't judge a book by its cover!" They both responded.

Chapter Thirteen

GIVE IT UP

I bet you thought that I was gonna give it up,

I bet you thought that I was gonna give it up.

But now I look at you and you're lookin' really blue,

Because I caught you wearin' someone else's shoes,

I bet you thought that I was gonna give it up.

Just have some pride and dignity cause' you got caught in the
act,

I knew something was off my heart was never fully intact.

And now you come around and you batt those pretty eyes

Then try to hide your lies under all of that disguise

I bet you thought that I was gonna give it up.

You need to accept that you were wrong and that you were at

fault

No situation is made better with a wound filled up with salt.

We can at least be civil and maybe even be friends

As long as you tell the truth and help me make amends

I bet you thought that I was gonna give it up.

I bet you thought that I was gonna give it up,

I bet you thought that I was gonna give it up.

But now I look at you and you're lookin' really blue,

Because I caught you wearin' someone else's shoes,

I bet you thought that I was gonna give it up.

What happened is in the past and I have forgiven you

Yet you still walk around and you're lookin really blue.

And now you call me up and ask to go for a ride

Has this taught you the grass isn't greener on the other side?

I bet you thought that I was gonna give it up.

Everyone makes mistakes don't beat yourself up too hard,

And make sure to mow the grass in your own yard.

I know I've moved on and I promise that we

Were never ever really even meant to be.

I bet you thought that I was gonna give it up,

I bet you thought that I was gonna give it up.

But now I look at you and you're lookin' really blue,

Because I caught you wearin' someone else's shoes,

I bet you thought that I was gonna give it up.

Use this as a tool and always remember this

Honesty is the best policy then seal it with a kiss.

We will never be more than friends I will not re-up

And now I'm gonna let you and give it up.

I stared at the picture that I had in black and white, printed from the security cameras at the studio. I could undoubtedly see Raven, Enzi, and Enid Rasp tampering with my car. It's like the *knew* that the camera was watching as they glared directly into the lens and smiled. I don't know what it is about Enid Rasp, but she makes me apprehensive about so many things—cautious concern.

"I made a new friend yesterday…" I contentedly told mom as she smiled deeply.

"Ooh, do tell…" She said.

"It is a new singer; his name is *also* Charles." I excitedly exclaimed. "We're going to try and collaborate on something. He just went through a serious break up. They were together for three years. So, I wrote a song for his situation." I said as I clutched the black and white picture in my hands and held it against my chest. I thumbed through the pages of music notes and lyrics until I found the song.

"I call it "Give It Up." I said as I handed it to her. She read it aloud and smiled, genuinely. "Words without music are nothing more than poems written from the heart, doomed to die when you do, but when you add music…then it begins to come from the soul, and it lives forever." I recited those words as mom put down the notebook and looked me in the eyes, gazing deep into my soul.

"Oh, that's beautiful honey, did you come up with that?" She asked. I gave her a puzzled look and cocked a half smile.

"Grandma told me that. She had to have told you all these motivational and inspirational things, didn't she?" I asked. She looked at me deeper, as if a sharp pain had suddenly stabbed her in the heart. "I know this look…" I thought to myself. "…Regret."

"If there is one thing I could take back…" She began to say as she paused to collect her words. "It would be to believe and to listen. All she wanted was to be heard…and I dismissed her." She sighed deeply, profoundly, and then shook the feelings away and forced a smile. "…Anyways, I love this song. Will you use a piano?" I nodded a yes as the coffee machine dripped its last drop, the aroma of Sumatra dancing around the room as we both smiled and enjoyed the miasma of a fresh morning.

Charles loved the song and it instantly resonated with him as he hummed the melody for *Give It Up*.

"Your reputation precedes you." He said.

"Hmmm, I have an idea." I said to him as if I were suddenly struck with genius instruction.

"I'm all ears." He said as he gave his ear a slight tug and laughed.

"This time…" I began to say, "…we both go in the booth." He looked at me, eyes overflowing with vigilant curiosity.

"A duo?" He asked.

"A duo." I said confidently.

"Alright, queue up guys, take one." I hollered to the engineers in the booth as I secured my headphones on my head. I watched as they played back the music and gave us a thumbs up. Three harmonious minutes and eighteen symphonic seconds later, we had a new number one hit. I looked at Charles as he looked at me—chests rising and falling—and we began to bellow in laughter.

"Did we just make a hit?" He asked. I smiled and nodded my head. "We need a name, after all, we are a duo, right?" I smiled and nodded, angling my head slightly and looked up as if the answer were on the ceiling of the soundproof booth that we both were sitting in. We needed a name that would catch and hold, something clever and creative.

"How about The Onesies'?" He playfully suggested.

"I like it, but I think that name implies there are more than two…" I told him as he agreed, and we brainstormed some more.

We played the song for Ripp and he elatedly approved as he obnoxiously applauded.

"We gotta get this out as fast as we can…on the radio. How about Charles squared?" Ripp suggested to us as a name for our group. At the same time both of our eyes lit up. It seemed so apparent, yet we couldn't come up with it on our own.

"Charles and Charles!" We both shouted in unison. Ripp smiled.

"Welcome to the team." He said as he offered to represent Charles, as his manager.

It was just past eight when Rip ran back inside from the rear parking lot where he was feeding his lungs with carcinogenic toxic fumes—cigarettes. Charles and I were fine tuning our song Give *It Up* when Ripp suddenly shouted.

"Charles! Someone just crawled out from underneath your car!" I looked at him, hoping that it was the other Charles and not me.

"What do you mean? Did you get a good look at the guy?" I asked, sleuth-like.

"You mean 'did I get a look at the *girl*'." He surprisingly said. "There were three of them; one was *very* skinny with hair like boiled spaghetti noodles." He said. I thought back through my rolodex of memory files.

"Was her hair the color of hay? Like a yellow-ish?" I asked.

"Yes! And I swear one of them may have been Raven. I called out her name and she looked up, anxiously."

"Thanks, Ripp." I said as I called mom and asked her to pick me up. "We can call it a night, everyone." I said as everyone agreed and collected their belongings and left. "Ripp…" I began to ask, "…Does this building have security cameras in the parking lot?"

"Yes." He said as he led me down the hall into the security room and showed me how to operate the systems.

"Finally!" I exclaimed as I found the frame and time stamp that I was looking for. It *was* Raven, Enzi and Enid Rasp and they had cut my brakes and carved something on the driver's side door. I zoomed in as far as I possibly could and then printed the screen in black and white. I finally had proof to give to mom so that she could see that this is a growing issue and that we *must* do something. They really were trying to kill me, or maybe kill us.

My phone buzzed as mom sent me a text message to let me know that she was waiting for me. I closed the building and locked the door. as I walked outside, mom was already standing at my driver's side door, staring at the strange markings that had been carved by key into the cardinal red paint on my car. It was an upside down cross with a blue diamond in the direct center that had a blood smeared fingerprint pressed into it.

"Charles, what is all of this?" She asked. "And what is this fluid I am standing in?" I crouched down and I drug my index finger through the puddle of liquid that was pooling underneath my car. I held my finger up to my nose and inhaled deeply.

"Smells like brake fluid." I told her. "Something isn't right, let's get out of here. It's dangerous." I said as we jumped in her SUV and quickly left.

As I sat in the front seat—my body melting and then amalgamating into the creamy leather—I studied the fluid that had stained my fingerprint. My skin was saturated with the tinge of brake fluid. The safety and security of having brake fluid in a working car is something that millions of people take for granted. It can save your life. But as I further studied the miscellany that soaked my skin, just a simple match or a spark could end it all. This one thing that could keep us alive is the same thing that could kill me.

"A metaphor for my life." I thought to myself.

"Enzi…" Enid Rasp shouted as they watched mom and I drive away. "You said he would drive *his* car home!" Enzi looked at her, ashamed.

"I thought he would…I didn't think he would call my mom. I'm sorry Enid Rasp!" Enzi pleaded. Enid Rasp looked at her with eyes full of trepidation.

"This better not happen again. This is your family we're trying to kill. You need to do better. Otherwise, you will *never* reach enlightenment." She said as Raven just sat in the back seat, laughing. Raven had been given a hit of acid earlier and it was still in its effects as she looked out the front windshield—that appeared to be melting—to see what she thought were bugs tap dancing.

"Do you guys see this? Are you guys seeing this?" Raven asked with eyes wide like an owls' and two giant black olives in her eyes. "You guys...there is a bug on the windshield and it's asking me to spit on him." She said as she began to gather saliva in her mouth. "Does anyone have any ketchup? It makes me spit better..." She said. Enid Rasp looked at Enzi and shook her head in disappointment.

"I figured she wouldn't be able to handle acid. What a waste!" Enid Rasp told her. "...Never again will I waste a hit on her. Get your girl under control before she comes up on the blotter as the next to be killed." Enzi looked at her, dejectedly, and crawled into the back seat.

"Here...just rest your head and be quiet. Please!" She begged Raven as she laid her head down and began to sleep.

Enid Rasp closely followed mom and me as I explained to her what happened and then I handed her the physical proof that they were trying to harm us. Mom—refusing the hard evidence and reality—changed the subject.

"We'll talk about this when I get you home." She said as she turned up the volume. Why was she still protecting them, I wondered to myself? Well, if mom won't listen to me, I knew one person who would: dad…and his gun.

Chapter Fourteen

There's a love I feel inside that I just cannot hide, this is it, this is it.

Oh, your love I will abide just to take you for a ride, this is it, this is

it.

I sat at the table, cyclically singing those words which seemed to materialize out of nowhere as I listened to the grinding of ingredients from the blender as it whirred, noisily at mom's command.

"What are you working on now?" Mom asked as she salted the rims of the glasses before she poured the frosty margaritas into it. "Your dad is ten minutes away." She said. I Looked at her and deeply smiled in eagerness, anticipating the mouth-watering frosted liquid which would whet my whistle.

"These words just came to me, appearing in my head as if they were scrolling on a teleprompter." I told her as I kept trying to write more. I Tried to rhyme more words and phrases together as my phone began to ring; I Looked down to see that it was dad calling me.

"Charles, where is your mother?" He asked, frantically.

"She just went out to the garden to gather some mint." I told him. "Why, what's going on?"

"I am by the barn…" He began to say fretfully, "…And I just found Enzi's truck parked behind it. She's not in it." My palms began to sweat, and my hands began to tremble, something didn't feel right. There was a portentous sensation in the air, almost like a warning.

"Dad, do you have your gun?" I asked as I ran outside to find mom. I got just within sight of her as she fell to the ground—cradling her head—writing in agony. Enid Rasp and Enzi stood behind mom; Enzi held a tire iron in her hands. I grabbed the nearest blunt object—a steel rake—and took up a defensive stance over mom. I looked deep into Enzi's eyes; she was unrecognizable with her pupils dilated—black as olives—undoubtedly, she was on drugs. She was white knuckling the tire iron. Enid Rasp tried to rush at me as she screamed to make me lose my focus.

"Finish her…you *HAVE* to finish her!" I rotated the rake and struck Enid Rasp in the side of her head with the flat part of the rake. Enzi was frozen in place, too scared to move, as Enid Rasp yelled at me.

"ASSHOLE! You tore part of my ear off!" Blood was gushing out of the tear in the side of her head.

"Mom…get up…you have to get up!" I pleaded.

"Enzi…you have to finish her. Finish her!" Enid Rasp yelled. Mom stumbled to her feet and began to hobble to the house, still holding her head which was throbbing with pain.

"Call the cops and lock the doors. Don't worry about me!" I shouted as I grabbed the rake with both hands—like a Louisville slugger—and swung at Enzi, warning her to stay back.

"You don't understand, Charles, I have to do this. You can't stop us!" Enzi breathlessly shouted. "It has to be done!" I noticed that Enzi was about to help Enid Rasp to her feet, so I shoved Enzi away and delivered a swift kick to Enid Rasps' solar plexus. She held her stomach—gasping for air like a fish out of water—and her face was speckled in blood like they were freckles in the sun. I stood guard as dad finally pulled up and saw me standing between the front door and these two.

"Where's your mother?!" Dad shouted as he pulled his gun out and loaded a round into the chamber.

"She is locked inside. The police are on the way. She's hurt!" I told him as I crammed him with information.

"Enzi, what the hell is the matter with you, I Told you that girl was no good!" He told her with resentment and disappointment swirling into a cloud just over his head.

"I'm sorry, daddy!" Enzi said as she began to sob loudly. Enid Rasp picked her face up from out of the soil and glared at Enzi.

"Don't apologize to him. Remember… E-N-L-I-G-H-T-E-N-M-E-N-T." Enzi said. Enzi stopped weeping and wiped the tears away as she turned to stone—no emotions.

"We can still finish this. Think of the money…think of the enlightenment!" Enid Rasp said as dad looked down at her in shame.

"But you are on the ground, in pain. And I am the one with the gun." He told her, arrogantly. I looked at the window and noticed mom standing at the kitchen sink looking out the window, giving a play-by-play to the 911 operator.

"That may be the case…" Enid Rasp began to say through infuriated breaths. "…But you locked her inside. Did you really think it would be just the two of us?" Her words filled me with fear as I could see the door behind mom slowly creeping open.

"Mom! Behind you!" I yelled. "Dad...mom..." I shouted even louder as dad turned his attention to the window that mom was looking out. "Grandma, please help!" I begged. It's as if grandma was present for the whole episode as all the morning glories snapped open and shut and open and shut, repeatedly—like umbrellas in a rainstorm. The vines from the morning glories began to unwind their vines and creep through the cracks in the window, defending mom. A throng of lightning bugs, thick like a dark rain cloud, began to swarm and crawl all over Enzi and Enid Rasp. It all happened so fast, yet it was in slow motion as the vines wrapped around Tillie, Raven and another member of The Mystic Mile who I had never seen before, a male with orange hair and pallid white skin—fish belly white.

The lightning bugs were keeping Enid Rasp and Enzi completely preoccupied, as they swatted them away, more flew in. Off in the distance, I could see a dust cloud, glowing red and blue. I ran inside, moms head was cradled in dads' hands as she cried. Raven and Tillie—wrapped in morning glories and unable to move—began to plead with us as the unidentified man, armed only with a large knife, cut his way out of the vines and ran out the back door into the forest.

"Charles, you don't understand." Raven began to say. "...I love you. Please don't let them take us!"

She loves me, I asked myself as I paused. My face was undisturbed, and I sympathetically looked deep into her eyes. It felt so good to hear those words coming from her once soft lips. I still loved her, after all, but she was different now. She was ominous, infected by the sisterhood.

"I love you too Raven. The old you. But you tried to kill me...tried to kill my family!" I said as I fought back tears. "I don't feel sorry for you!" My eyes glossed over as the cops finally arrived, placing Enid Rasp and Enzi in handcuffs. The dark cloud of lightning bugs dissipated like a warning flare and stippled the air once more with their intermittent flickers of light—calming the air around all of us. They placed Enid Rasp and Enzi in the back of the squad car and came inside to get Tillie and Raven. The responding officers were taken back to see that Tillie and Raven were stuck to the wall like a fly stuck to a spider's web. All the colorful blooms were beaming bright purple and lavender blue hues and were facing Tillie and Raven as if they were keeping a vigilant petal on them. I looked at mom; her vision was hazy from all the tears.

"Grandma is here..." I told her. The police were blown away that nature, the morning glories, and lightning bugs, stopped an attack that could have been much worse. "There is still one more..." I began to tell another officer, "...He ran out the back door and into the woods. He is about five foot eight and has fire orange hair..." I said as I began to describe him, "...skin as white as snow." They wrote down the description and sent officers into the coppice. "Grandma...you can let them go now." I said as the vines began to recede and slowly crept back out the window to the trellis.

"What kind of plant is that?" One of the officers asked.

"If you ever come across a bit of magic, officer, it's best not to ask questions." Mom simply said. "I'm ready to give my statement...I'll tell you everything." Mom said as she picked up a morning glory—broken at the stem—and placed it behind her ears.

"Mom…" I began to say as she held up her hand, interrupting me.

"I know what you're going to say, Charles, but I am done protecting them. I will tell them everything, I promise." She said as I smiled. Dad sat next to her, fingers laced like shoelace, as the ambulance patched her up and she gave all the information to the officer.

I walked outside to the trellis, holding the I Love Lucy pendant in my hand, and dropped to my knees. I pulled back a handful of soil at the base of the trellis as all the morning glories faced downward, watching me. I placed the pendant in the freshly dug ground and buried the pendant. I Looked up and saw the blooms and began to count.

"Forty-seven." I said out loud. "Grandma, I don't even know how to thank you." I softly said as I wrapped my arms around the trellis, a chill on my skin as I pressed my face against the cold leaves. "I knew I could count on you." The leaves began to shake, as if they were crying to themselves.

"Poodle…" she began to whisper, "…Poodle." I smiled; her voice always gave me such solace.

"I'm here, grandma." I told her.

"I know you're here…I was building suspense. Silly boy!" She said in jest—a fool to lighten the doldrums. "You tell your mother to always trust her gut. It's the only thing that will always be with her." I smiled as I stood up and brushed the soil from my knees. When I looked at the forty-seventh bloom—the biggest bloom, in fact—the I Love Lucy pendant was hanging there as if it were being worn on a lapel. The petals closed one by one until they were all closed. I turned around to see the setting sun over the thicket. The substantial tinge of orange, purple, gray and red outlined the sky as it seemed set on fire by the arrival of the moon.

"Good night, grandma."

Chapter Fifteen

There is nothing more delightfully evocative than lightning during a hurricane. The commanding display of nature's fury, showing us just how diminutive and inconsequential we really are in this world.

I sat next to the window watching the flashes of lightning as they danced across the sky.

"One Mississippi…two Mississ—" I began to count as a large, echoing clap of thunder shook the lead paned windows, jolting me out of my daydream. Two days ago, the world was introduced to *Charles & Charles*: the newest addition to the Billboard Top 200. My first single, *Forgiveness Train*, was re-released under our name, making it number one and number 4. Charles and I *finally* finished the album-which was set to be released at the end of the month— however, Ripp pushed the release to a later date until after the first court hearing for Tillie and Enzi.

"This wait will just garner you more fans and attention." Ripp happily said with dollar signs in his eyes. "Focus on your family and personal life...just don't do anything stupid."

I stood up from the chair next to the window, annoyed that the crows weren't trying to steal the eggs from the red birds. "Come on...do something...anything!" I shouted as I slammed my naked hands against the window—the red birds staring at me with condemnatory eyes.

"Oh look, that is the guy who imprisoned his own sisters...his own blood!" The birds must be thinking to one another.

"Shut up! You don't know what you're squawking about!" I unexpectedly shouted. My chest was rising and falling, and my blood was pumping fast as I caught a glimpse of my reflection in the window, until my warm, humid breath replaced it with fog.

"This is what I've become..." I mumbled to myself as I walked down the stairs and to the front door, flinging it open. I stood there, listening to the rhythm of the rain, wondering if this is what applause sounded like. I looked over at the morning glories, the leaves were flinching with every drop of rain that landed on them.

"Grandma, are you there?" I asked. The forty-seventh bloom—the biggest of them all—opened and turned to face me. I stepped out of the doorway as a sheet of water doused me from head to toe, filling my shoes with water. "Grandma, did I do the right thing?" I asked, insecurities once again slowly taking over.

"Poodle, you never know until you know...but when you know you know, ya' know?" She said. I smiled softly; her conundrum really hit home for me. It was the perfect balance of a nonsensical idiom that somehow battled my doubt and uncertainty. She was right, you never know until you know, and I had to trust in my gut instinct and see this through to the end.

"Thank you, grandma." I said through chattering clenched teeth as the blossom snapped shut.

I walked into the kitchen and noticed that there was a canary yellow post-it note stuck to the fridge. *Dinner at 5:30, don't be late,* it read. I hard-pressed the brew button on the coffee maker and cracked open a window, inviting the rainstorm inside. It was nearly noon and I had time to kill; I just didn't want to do anything. I wanted to evaporate into the Ever After where grandma is, just to see what it was like in there.

"Maybe I could become a mighty oak tree…or even a weeping willow, offering shade and comfort for generations to come…" I began to tell myself. "Or maybe a babbling creek, that way when I talk to someone I could do it through their own reflection, making them feel saner than a person who is actively talking to a creek." I stood there for a moment—picturing myself as a creek—wondering how many bends I would have. Would I have a strong current—like the blood rushing through my veins—or a mild one. "I know what I can do." I triumphed. It was my first eureka moment in many, many months.

I walked into the spare bedroom and pulled open the top dresser drawer as it fell off the tracks. I had to push it back in and realign it before I could pull it out all the way. There, staring at me, were all of grandma's treasures just waiting to be dusted off and hidden throughout the house. I had an arbitrary burst of energy that had been vacant since before that unpleasant incident. Like it got hauled away in handcuffs with Tillie and Enzi…and Raven too. I hid every treasure throughout the house, a smile painted across my face like the Mona Lisa.

"There…all finished. Good luck!" I said as I opened all the windows and went upstairs to shower and get ready.

I came down the stairs an hour later, dressed, and ready for dinner. Mom and dad called this dinner, inviting Trevor, Sean, and me. No doubt to discuss Enzi and Tillie. They are our little sisters, after all. And yes, I love them, but this was the second time that they tried to kill us.

"Damn you Enid Rasp!" I shouted as I walked into the kitchen to see all of grandma's treasures skillfully placed, side by side, on the granite countertop next to a freshly picked morning glory. I smiled as I poured a hot cup of coffee—black as coal—and walked over to the window. "I guess I will have to try harder…" I said to the rain. I looked down at the morning glory, it was so luminous and purple like an amethyst struck by a ray of sun. It was too purple to be real, like it was digitally enhanced, however, the unrealistic purple flower brought calmness to my nerves.

"You're in charge." I said to the morning glory as I finished my coffee. I grabbed my keys, wallet and headed for the front door. I Turned around and placed the morning glory on the ground in front of the door. "Hold down the fort." I said as I shut the door behind me and locked it. As I walked to my car, I passed the trellis of morning glories and quickly looked at the I Love Lucy pendant and smiled as it hung off the forty-seventh bloom, swaying like a pendulum in the storm. It's difficult to describe the way that a morning glory smiles, but I want *that* to be the last thing I see before I depart this earth and join those in the Ever After.

I parked my car between Sean and Trevor's vehicles and got out of my car the same time they got out of theirs.

"Hey guys." I said as I hugged them—brotherly love.

"Charles…do you know what this is about?" Trevor asked. I shrugged my shoulders—a convincing lie as I was almost positive what the theme of the night would be.

"Your guess is as good as mine." I said. I think we *all* knew what this was about, and it was a topic that all of us wanted to steer clear of at all costs.

"Boys!" Mom shouted as she greeted each of us with a warm and affable hug and kiss. She and dad were moving around the house quickly, as if they were running behind schedule. I inhaled deeply—nothing.

"Mom, where is dinner?" I asked.

"Yeah…" Trevor began to say as he held his stomach. "…I am starving." Mom looked over at dad and then at all of us.

"What is going on?" Sean asked. "C'mon, out with it."

"Boys, your father and I have dinner plans. We just called you over to tell you that the prosecutors have reached a deal with Tillie and Enzi. Your sisters pleaded temporary insanity…" She said, pausing to push away a fit of disturbance. "…They are being moved to Green Acre's, where they will be admitted for the next three and a half years." She shook her head in disappointment.

"We tried to appeal and ask for a trial, but we were shot down." Dad said. "We're going to sign the transfer paperwork right now." I was livid and I wanted to scream. "I know what you're thinking, Charles, but hopefully they can be rehabilitated." Dad dejectedly said as he looked at me and then placed his hand on my shoulder.

"What will happen to Enid Rasp and Raven?" I asked.

"Raven had never been in trouble up until now, so she was released with a slap on the wrist. And that monster, Enid Rasp, will also be admitted to Green Acres." Mom said, her hands trembling as I reached over and held them.

"They are keeping them all together. This…this…this is ludicrous!" I shouted. Sean and Trevor were just standing there, mystified. They weren't present for any of this, so I understood their detachment.

"This isn't ideal, boys, but we have to just trust that the courts know what they are doing. I love you all…but your father and I are running late." She said as she and dad walked towards their car. Sean and Trevor walked to theirs.

"Call us and tell us how it goes?" I hollered. Mom smiled and nodded as she shut her door.

I thought back to the conundrum that grandma hit me with earlier: *You never know until you know, but when you know you know, ya' know?* I smiled and got into my car, gripping my steering wheel.

I trust you." I said out loud as I flipped on the radio. The announcer was speaking to her audience.

"Up next, 'Forgiveness Train', by Charles & Charles." I turned up the volume to the highest decibel and absorbed the feeling that was coursing through my veins.

"Anything could happen…" I considered. "…Anything could happen."

Chapter Sixteen

Two idealistically perfect weeks had gone by before the silence became too much for mom; she called Dr. Spar at Green Acre's to check on Tillie and Enzi.

"Don't look at me like that, Charles, they are still my daughters. Family doesn't quit on each other." She scolded as we sat in the kitchen drinking freshly brewed coffee as the wind blew in an ominous wail. "Dr. Spar, hello, I am calling to check on Tillie and Enzi Ponder, this is their mother Evonne." She said as we listened to the loud gulping of liquid as Dr. Spar washed down the half-masticated bite of club sandwich that he was having for lunch.

"Mmhmm…I am glad that you called Mrs. Ponder. They are sensational, to say the least. I have entirely nothing negative to report, which, as you can imagine, I almost never get to say in my line of work." He genially stated as if they were his high-quality pupils on the Dean's list, and he was the Dean.

"Just give it time…" I mumbled loudly. Mom just cut me a look and pursed her lips together tightly.

"That's great to hear. They always were such good girls…I think they were just manipulated and confused by that Enid Rasp…that girl is just awful—" Mom stated as Dr. Spar began to shout.

"HEY, WATCH YOUR MOUTH!" Silence fell over both ends of the phone call for a moment before he cleared his throat. "Mrs. Ponder, I apologize. You see, here at Green Acre's, we believe that everyone is intrinsically good…so we don't allow name calling of *any* kind." I looked at mom as she held her finger up in a scolding manner as if to silently san: *Don't say a word, boy!* "Enid is doing just as good, if not better. I see real rehabilitative potential in all three, and they are all just simply inseparable." He said, further twisting the knife into the open wound of my impatience.

"WE DON'T CARE ABOUT HOW WELL ENID RASP IS DOING!" I shouted.

"Charles…please…" mom begged. "I apologize, Dr. Spar, we're still working through some things." Mom explained as I threw up my hands, grabbed my cup of coffee and walked out of the room.

"If they keep up the good work, I may even recommend an earlier release. No point in keeping patients here for any longer than they need to be. After all, there are some *demented* individuals out there who could benefit from their slots." He said as he chuckled, vaguely. "I have scheduled a phone call for them to call you this Thursday at eleven, will that work for you?" He asked. Mom looked around the room, reticently.

"Yes." She whispered as she hung up the phone.

"I don't know what that guy's deal is, dad, but I will take care of him!" Enid Rasp threatened as she slammed her fists down onto Dr. Spar—her fathers—desk.

"In due time, Enid, in due time." He said as he ran his fingers through her hair. "And you two…" He said as he pointed to Enzi and Tillie. "You two will soon reach Enlightenment, I can feel it. I have informed The Mystic Miles' brethren to keep a watchful eye on everyone. When they have finally forgotten, that is when we will strike." He said, his professional eyes growing more and more sinister the wider he smiled.

"But how long will we have to wait, dad?" Enid Rasp asked, impatiently.

"As long as we must, Enid. Until then, the three of you will remain locked here under my watch and you will be on your best behavior. Am I understood?" He asked.

"Yes sir…" They all replied in perfect unison.

Ripp called Charles and I into the studio, out of the blue. "This could either be really good or really bad." I thought to myself as I put my car into park and walked up to the side door of the studio, waiting for security to buzz me in. I walked up the stairs and found Charles making a cup of coffee for himself.

"Hey, you got here fast!" I said, happy to see him. He nodded as the piping hot liquid scolded the taste buds right off his tongue, burning his mouth.

"There they are…my shining stars!" Ripp elatedly praised. "Come in." I grabbed myself a cup of coffee and joined Charles on the comfortable leather sofa. "So, listen guys, this is about our re-release of Forgiveness Train." He began to say.

"Is there a problem with it?" I asked.

"Well no, technically not, it's still hovering at the top. It's just the same title as the song you wrote for Ellipses…" He said as he pointed at me, mid sip.

"Excuse me? It just has the same title, but Charles and I wrote an entirely new song based off our interpretation of that title." I began to spew words out of my mouth like an oil spill, clearly Ripp struck a nerve.

"Well, Ellipses thinks you were holding out on her is all…" Ripp watchfully said.

"Well, screw her!" I shouted. "I wrote that song for her. I helped her get her first number one hit…and now she is jealous that Charles and I are rising higher than her on the charts?" Ripp looked at me warily as he carefully picked his next words.

"So…asking you guys to at least change the title is not going to happen, is it?" He asked. Charles—who had been silent this entire time—finally blew his fuse as he looked at me and then over to Ripp, his face scrunched in annoyance.

HELL NO!" He vigorously shouted. "…And if she isn't careful, we will take all of the titles from her new album and write better songs based off them. Between Charles and me, we can do it and we can do it better." I looked at Charles and then over to Ripp with a satisfied smirk across my face.

"I stand by my bandmate." I said. Ripp smiled and interlaced his fingers together like a Native American quilt and rested them lightly on his large oak desk.

"That would be a PR nightmare, but I don't doubt your ambition boys." He said.

"Ripp…" I began to say softly, "…Does Ellipses know just how many songs in existence bear the same title?" I asked.

"I don't think so, but she will soon find out if she doesn't cool her jets. I stand behind you boys." Ripp said as he smiled and looked around the room. He opened the bottom right drawer and pulled out a blood red folder labeled: *Charles & Charles*. "Now, about the album release…" He barked as he looked at the both of us. Ripp paused for a long, dramatic effect as Charles and I sat on the edge of our seats, holding onto every bit of silence that dripped off his lips.

"What! Tell us!" Charles shouted. Ripp laughed as he straightened a stack of papers on his desk and slammed the blood red folder down.

"You two, together, are going to be colossal! It's going to be released tonight at midnight. So, drink plenty of coffee and stay awake!" He happily stated as Charles and I looked at each other, teeming with anticipation. "Once we figure out how the sales go, we can negotiate…" he said as he pointed at Charles, "…And re-negotiate…" He said, pointing at me, "…Your contracts." Charles and I looked at each other and smiled even wider.

"Fifty-fifty?" I asked, looking at Ripp and raising one eyebrow.

"…Of course…" He said, "…Now why don't the two of you celebrate together tonight. Charles, why don't you go over to Maple Creek Farm?" Ripp suggested as he looked at me.

"Actually, that's a great idea." I said, smiling. "You'll love it, it's magical there!" He smiled admiringly.

"I can't wait. I have an overnight bag in my trunk." He said.

"So, it is settled…" Ripp elatedly belted. "I'll see the two of you in a few days, keep your phones on you."

I sat in my car and drafted a text message to mom, dad, Sean and Trevor as I patiently waited for Charles to get his things. *Guys, tonight at midnight our new album drops!* Charles opened the door to the back seat and plopped his overnight bag down onto the cold leather seat.

"I am so excited!" He said. "Ripp told me about your recent renovation…it was your grandparents' house, no?" He asked.

"Yes. And I can't wait to introduce you to my grandma, she's a hoot!" I happily told him. He studied my eyes and my facial movements for a moment before he cleared his throat.

"Umm…Charles?" He stammered. "Didn't she pass away?" He asked. I sat there for a moment, speechless. Yes, technically grandma did die, but did she? Yes, she was cremated, but the moment she lost her physical form she became something more. I looked over at Charles at a loss for words.

"Uhm. Well, as my grandma used to say, when you encounter a bit of magic, don't ask questions." I said. He smiled and reached over and put his hand on mine and gave it a minor squeeze as I rested it on the gear shifter.

"I can respect that." He said as he quickly pulled his hand off mine. "P.S. we are *never* writing anything for Ellipses ever again, deal?" He asked.

"Deal!" I happily said as I turned up the volume on the radio just in time to hear the beginning instrumentals for our song. Charles and I looked at each other and began to laugh.

Chapter Seventeen

It had been a long time—well over a year—since the last time that I had invited a visitor to this house that wasn't family. Sure, there is Ripp Carnegie, but he may as well be family. He has been with me for nearly ten years—my longest relationship.

"You're right, this place is magical." Charles said as I showed him around the house. "It's beautiful, like out of a story book." He said as he sauntered into the kitchen. "And the updates are tasteful. You picked the perfect slab of granite to compliment the colors in here…" He contentedly said as he paused and pointed at the kitchen sink. "…and this copper sink?" He asked. I smiled as I opened the refrigerator and pulled out a bottle of chilled champagne and grabbed two champagne flutes.

"Grandma always loved that copper sink…" I said as I smiled. "I guess I couldn't bring myself to modernize everything." I said.

"Good choice, this sink brings the entire room to life." He competently stated, like he knew a thing or two about remodeling houses. I gave him a puzzled look as he began to laugh. "Sorry, my dad owns his own construction company. He mainly builds and remodels, so I grew up helping him on different job sites." He said as he ran his finger along the carvings in the cupboards. "You do all the work by yourself?" He asked. I looked out the window—the same one mom and grandma looked out—and I smiled slightly as I opened the window.

"My dad, my brothers and I did it over the summer." I said.

"Well, y'all did a really good job. Exceptionally clean lines." He said.

"We wanted to make grandma and grandpa proud…" I said as I filled up the tea kettle with water. "Coffee or tea?"

"Tea for now…so when do I get to meet your grandma?" He asked as I looked down at my watch.

"Soon, the sunset—" I said as I pointed out the window. "Come with me."

We walked out the front door and walked out to the fence that was blanketed in morning glories, the place where grandma and I found grandpa.

"Tell me what you smell…" I told him as I reached down and plucked a morning glory and carefully held it between my fingertips as I twisted the stem back and forth, making it twirl. Charles inhaled profoundly as he closed his eyes and smiled. "…Good memory?" I asked.

"Yes, it smells like strawberries." He began to say.

"And what memory comes to mind?" I asked.

"…When I was young, seven years old to be exact, I was riding my bike near the farmers market when, out of nowhere, an exceptionally large dog began to chase me. I was so scared, and I began to pedal harder than I ever have before. The harder I pedaled the harder I cried. At some point I was crying so hard that I Rode my bike right into a curb and flew right over the handlebars. That was when the dog latched his jaws, sank his teeth into my leg, and vigorously pulled like we were playing tug-of-war." He said as he pulled up his pants and showed me the scar. "I was bleeding, but I knew that I had to get away, so I kicked the dog in the face, really hard. He yelped. I got to my feet and began to run through the aisles of the farmers market until I reached a table selling fresh strawberries…and then I hid under the table. A strawberry rolled off the table and I reached out and grab bed it. I stared at it and just stopped crying, almost like it took away all of my fear." He said as he looked deep into my eyes, studying me like a test. "Know what I mean?"

"I do." I told him.

"Anyways, the wind began to blow and there was a voice. A beautiful voice that told me to eat the strawberry, so I did. Immediately all the pain went away. the blood disappeared and the dog bite healed into a scar, right before my eyes." He said. A smile beamed across his face. "I probably sound crazy, don't I?" He asked, tepid with embarrassment.

"No, not at all. I totally believe you…" I told him as I reached down and grab bed his hand. "…I think it's time for you to meet grandma…" I said as I led him to the trellis where the barrage of morning glories rested their tired petals. I pointed to the morning glories as he stepped closer, squinting his eyes.

"Is…is your grandma the lady from the I Love Lucy show?" He asked as he looked at the I Love Lucy pendant that hung on the largest bloom, suspended. I laughed and stepped closer to the morning glories.

"No…grandma, are you there?" I asked as the leaves began to rustle and shudder as all the blooms opened and began to stretch their petals—a good days sleep. Charles looked at me, eyes wide like they were that day at the farmers market when he was seven. He reached down and grabbed my hand. "It's okay." I told him.

"Poodle…look at that…would you just look at that sunset!" She said as we turned just in time to see the sky catch fire with an explosion of orange, red and purple.

"Beautiful…" I said as Charles just smiled.

"Poodle, did he ask if I was Lucille Ball?" Grandma asked, laughing. "That woman was *much* older than me." I laughed slightly and shook my head.

"Charles, meet grandma…grandma…" I said as I nudged Charles closer to the trellis. "…This is Charles…" Charles smiled deeply as he curtsied. "Did you just—?" I began to ask as grandma finished my sentence.

"Did he just curtsy me?" Grandma asked, shaking her leaves in laughter.

"Yeah, I kind of panicked. When in doubt, offer an obeisance. It's nice to meet you…" He said as he looked at me. He peered over my shoulder, into the thicket of the forest, with curious eyes as he squinted. "Who is that?" Charles asked as he pointed towards the coppice.

"Who is who?" I asked. He grabbed my hand and led me over to the fence and pointed at an opening.

"I just saw a man, dressed in all black, with red hair, standing there. I think he was on the phone." He told me as I studied the area for movement.

"Hmmm…well, let's go inside." I suggested. "Grandma, keep a watchful eye please." I said as we walked past the trellis and went inside.

"You fool!" Dr. Spar shouted over the speaker of the phone that sat on his desk. "Were you seen?" He asked.

"No, I don't think so…" The man from The Mystic Mile responded as he scratched liberally at his legs. "I'm sorry sir; I think I knelt down in poison ivy…" He said as Dr. Spar slammed his fists down onto the desk.

"Don't screw this up. If this plan goes to hell and falls through just because of a little poison ivy, I will have you hung upside down and gutted!" Dr. Spar spat. "Am I understood?"

"Yes, sir!" He dejectedly responded as he hung up the phone.

Dr. Spar picked up his phone and dialed Raven's phone number.

"Raven, it is I. Your next step of Enlightenment is this: figure out who this new guy is that Charles is hanging out with and push him away from Charles. Flirt with him. Hell, sleep with him if you have too. Just make sure you separate the two!" He said as Raven began to jot down notes for her next mission.

"Yes sir. It will be done!" Raven submitted as she hung up the phone.

Chapter Eighteen

"Poodle, happiness is real. It seeps deep into your skin. It is an overwhelming feeling unlike anything you've ever felt before, don't fight it." Grandma whispered that to me as I was in a deep slumber, bounded by shadows. I dreamt that we were trapped in my vehicle, upside down, floating down the river. I kept trying to reach for the window to roll it down, but the water was too freezing, and I couldn't move. I was the last to die. As I looked around, mom had her fingers laced through dad's fingers with a look of absolute fear in her eyes as water flooded her lungs. Dad, even in death, remained stoic; even as he gasped for his very last breath of air, he looked calm. Grandpa went first and grandma had a smile permanently etched on her face, complimented by patches of spaghetti sauce that the river eventually washed away, with the rest of us.

I sat up in bed, sweat beading down my back and forehead. I sat there, collecting my thoughts as I calmed myself down. I looked over at the chair as a single morning glory sat on the decorative pillow, spotlighted by the waxing moon.

"Hello." I said as I got out of bed, picked up the delicate morning glory and then sat in the chair. It smelled like grandma, I thought, as I held it under my nose and wafted in deeply.

I looked out the window as the moon flooded the fields with illumination, the type where you could easily navigate the darkest of paths with ease.

"Happiness is real...don't fight it..." I said out loud to myself. "Wonder what that means?"

I pondered the message that woke me from my night terror, and I couldn't stop thinking about it. Not until I looked out the window. The lightning bugs were lighting up the field in a way reminiscent to a disco ball.

"What in the hell—" I said as I pulled a shirt on and walked down the stairs and into the kitchen. I grabbed for my phone—which sat on the hard, glossy granite countertops—and checked the time; 3330 AM. I peered out the window next to the copper sink—the same mom and grandma peered out—and I noticed three hooded figures standing at the fence line next to the fields.

"A warning…" I thought as the lightning bugs flicked on and off with arbitrary bursts of fire. They stood there; watching me at the window as I stood there watching them at the fence. Their stillness made me anxious and tense, so I opened the window slightly and began to whisper into the night zephyrs.

"Grandma, are you there?" I asked.

"Yes, Poodle." The wind whistled quietly.

"Grandma, I need your help. Those people in black that are standing at the fence…" I said as I pointed to the spot where we found grandpa. I heard the gentle rustle of leaves and I just *knew* that grandma was on the case. My phone began to buzz and light up in my palm. "Charles…" I said as I read the name that displayed on the phone screen. I backed away from the window into the shadows and out of sight before I answered it.

"Charles…" I began to whisper, "…I need your help."

"What? I'm just down the road from your house. I didn't want to go home after deejaying at the club, so I started driving to your house." He said with a slight slur. I could tell he had tossed back a few drinks.

"Charles, I can see you. I need you to blare your horn like you're stuck in New York City traffic!" I shouted as I hurried back into the kitchen to watch the three figures dressed in black. Charles blared his horn and flashed his lights on and off and on and off. It appeared to alarm the three figures as they turned and ran through the fields, through the mine field of lightning bugs and into the cover of the coppice. I opened the door as Charles put the car in park and ran inside. I Locked the door behind him.

"Thank you so much!" I said as I threw my arms around him.

"What is going on?" He asked. He had a confused and bewildered look on his face and wasn't processing everything as fast as he usually does.

"There were these three figures standing at the fence line dressed in black robes. They were just staring at me as I was staring at them." I told him as I began to turn on all the lights in the house. "The sun should come up soon...coffee?" I asked.

"Mmmm, please..." He said. "I met the weirdest girl tonight at the club. I thought she was a reporter with the way she kept asking about you and me, our music, my relationship to you and even where you were tonight." I looked at him with a confused look on my face, but I was curious about this new person who had a sudden interest in us.

"What did you tell her?" I asked.

"Nothing really, just that you were at your house either writing another song or you were asleep. And then she asked if you were all alone at your house…I told her that, yes, you did live alone…" He said as he stopped talking about paused.

"Then what?" I asked.

"After I told her that, she said she had to go to the restroom, and she was gone for like ten minutes." He continued to say as he looked out the kitchen window towards the field. "You don't think that I…that she…?" He stammered as he began to put the pieces of the puzzle in the correct places, revealing the big picture.

"It's a strong possibility. The guy that you saw that day…the one dressed in all black…" I began to say as he interrupted me.

"I thought that you didn't believe me!" He said.

"I never said that I didn't believe you, I just said I didn't see him with *my* own eyes…but if it is any consolation, I believe you now." I told him as the coffee pot beeped and finished percolating. "…And this girl that you met…?" I asked.

"She said that her name was Nevar, at least that is what she saved it as when typed her number into my phone." He said as he pulled up her contact information and showed me.

"Ha! That's not even trying!" I said as I chuckled and shook my head.

"What do you mean?" He asked, slightly confused.

"Nevar is Raven spelled backwards. Raven just happens to be my ex-wife." I said as his eyes widened and his jaw nearly fell to the floor.

"One of the ones who tried to kill you and your family? So…I unknowingly gave her your location?" He asked, feeling guilty. I poured two cups of hot coffee as he grabbed one of them and then sat down. "I'm so sorry, Charles, I feel terrible. I swear I didn't know." He said.

"I know you didn't. I think she is trying to pick up where Tillie, Enzi and that Enid Rasp left off. I have to tell mom." I said as I text her and invited her over for breakfast.

"She tried to go home with me too. She got very mad when I declined her offer. She looked worried, like she was in trouble for not going home with me. It was weird." He said.

"They obviously didn't expect anyone to drive down that road." I told him, smiling. "You may have just saved my life." He laughed and took another sip of coffee and then looked deep into my eyes.

"I also might've been the reason they tried to kill you. If, that is, they could get past your grandma."

Charles made breakfast for the three of us and finished just as the sun peaked its rays over the hills and brought life to the fields once more. Mom arrived just as I pulled the fluffy, golden brown croissants out of the oven. I told mom everything that had transpired over the last two weeks, and then last night's occurrence. She smiled after she took a sip of fresh coffee.

"Album sales seem to be doing well…I subscribed to the Billboard magazine…" She began to say. "…You boys are still on top!" I scrunched my face and gave her a look full of disparagement; I never did like talking about myself.

"Yes, apparently our songs really seem to resonate with people." Charles happily said. "Another croissant?" He asked.

"No thank you dear…" She began to say as she shifted her weight in her chair and focused on me. "…So are you going to tell me what exactly is going on?"

"These people in black, mom, the robes…who do you think they are?" I asked. Charles and I sat at the table with her and began to explain everything. "And Raven… Charles, show mom the text messages." I said. Charles handed his phone to mom as she read the text messaging conversation between him and Raven. "Raven has been blowing up his phone pretending to be a girl called Nevar…" I told her as she interrupted.

"That's not even trying to disguise your name." She said as I laughed.

"That's exactly what he said!" Charles said as he laughed at the similarity between me and my mother.

"Anyways, somehow, I think it is all connected to Tillie, Enzi and Enid Rasp. I mean what do we actually know about The Mystic Mile?" I asked.

"Next to nothing, believe me I have asked." Mom said. "But when I spoke to the girls, they sounded so much better. Like they were themselves again…" I reached out and grabbed her hand and smiled through sympathetic eyes.

"Mom, it might be time for you to visit." I suggested. "If they are coming around here at night then they probably aren't too far from your house too." I told her. "We have to remain at least two steps ahead of them at all times…" I said as I looked at Charles. "…All of us." Mom nodded her head and smiled.

"I'll schedule a visit. If they think I am a fool, then that means they don't suspect anything. I will not let those girls try and harm anyone in our family." She said.

"Charles, you keep on texting Raven…ahem… I mean Nevar, figure out what she knows." I said as we all grabbed our cups of coffee and clanked them together in the air with a festive *Cheers*.

Chapter Nineteen

"Evonne, wherever there's a charmer, there is bound to be a snake."

Mom woke up from a mid-day nap with those words hovering around in her mind, like alphabet soup. "Hmm, odd…" She thought to herself as she got up from the couch where she had been napping and walked into the kitchen to make herself a cup of tea. She had been thinking about the plan that she had made earlier with Charles and I as she sat down with her cup of tea—phone in hand—ready to set an appointment to meet with Tillie and Enzi and set the plan into motion.

"Dr. Spar, hello, its Evonne Ponder." She said as she greeted him.

"Mrs. Ponder, to what do I owe the honor?" He asked. She took a deep breath, knowing that she was about to ask for an invitation into the lion's den.

"Well…" She began to say, "…I was hoping that I Could come and visit my girls." She let the words drip off her lips with just the smallest amount of flirtation; Dr. Spark picked up on it immediately.

"As long as you join me in my office for a drink…I do have questions which, I think, could aid in the rehabilitation of Tillie and Enzi…we are so close, after all." He said.

"Anything that might help me get my girls back sooner…" She began to say, "…How about four o' clock sharp?" She suggested.

"On the dot?" He asked.

"On the dot!" She happily said as she hung up the phone.

"…Well you heard it…" Dr. Spar said as Tillie and Enzi sat silently in his office listening to the conversation that he had with their mother.

"What's going to happen to her?" Tillie curiously asked.

"You girls just make her think you are better, convince her. I, on the other hand, am having drinks with her. I am going to slip something tasteless, odorless and completely undetectable into her drink. Poison. It will take a full week for it to fully kill her and it will be a slow and painful death. Then you two will be that much closer to enlightenment." He said as he walked over to Tillie and ran his rough hand down her face then pulled her close, removing the dead space between their lips. She trembled. He released and then pressed his lips against Enzi's lips. She didn't shudder. "Now go and get ready."

Mom called and told me about the weird message that she got while sleeping, and then continued to tell me of her conversation with Dr. Spar. Only Raven knew who Charles was and only she would recognize him, so he offered to drive mom.

"I'll wait right out front." He said to her as he pulled up to the front of the Green Acre's. Dr. Spar was standing at the foot of the steps, *right* at 4 o' clock sharp.

"I thought you would be coming alone…" He said as he greeted mom.

"Well…" Mom began to say as she quickly thought of an excuse, "…you mentioned drinks?" She asked sweetly as she fluttered her long, butterfly legged eye lashes. "I didn't want to drive if I was to be drinking." Dr. Spar smiled and nodded at Charles, clearly, he didn't recognize him.

They walked into the building, through a set of double doors, as a blast of chilly air slapped mom in the face.

"Oooh, well that is refreshing." She said.

"It's an old building, tends to get humid. Also, the cold air seems to calm the patients." He said as he opened his office door. "Please come in." Mom went in and surveyed her surroundings within a matter of seconds.

"A paperweight, scissors, a trophy…" She began to silently list things in her mind that she could possibly use as a weapon if things escalated. She was taken aback by the sheer size of his office. "There must be ten thousand books in here…" She said, astounded. Dr. Spar chuckled slightly and pulled out a chair for her to sit in.

"Ten thousand and one, to be exact. Please, sit." He said.

"Oh, so chivalrous." She flirted. He looked down at her from above as he pushed her chair in and noticed a deep lavender morning glory tucked behind her ear, staring him in the face.

"Pretty flower." He said.

"Thank you. It's a morning glory…they grow wild at my sons house." She said. He looked at her and smiled.

"What's your poison?" He asked. She smiled politely and made eye contact.

"Whiskey please." She sweetly said.

"Hmm, I had you pegged as a bourbon girl." He said, his back facing her. She smiled and didn't say anything. "So, Tillie and Enzi mentioned that the morning glories were alive…" He said—loud enough to cover up the sounds of treachery—as he reached inside his jacket pocket and grabbed a capsule and broke it in half, pouring the powder into her glass of whiskey. "But of course, I told them, that would be impossible…couldn't be backed up by scientific research." He said as he sat in the chair next to mom.

"Do you think the girls are clinically insane?" Mom began to ask as the morning glory quietly whispered to her: *Switch Drinks*. "Oh, that's a beautiful collection…" Mom said as she pointed behind him. His eyes lit up in admiration. He got up and walked over to the shadow box picture frame that held all his most prized collection of rare, historic stamps. While he had his back turned, she switched her glass for his. "I absolutely love vintage stamps. They just don't make them like they used to…cheers…" She slyly said.

"To the last drop." He said with his deep, baritone voice full of malice. She tossed back her drink and then licked her lips.

"Mmmm, great year!" She said as she got up and pretended to admire his collection.

She began to walk around his office, hoping that whatever was in the glass that he ingested—whatever had been intended for her—would kick in fast. She walked behind his desk and began to admire the pictures on his desk.

"Oh, is this your graduating class?" She asked as she held a frame that had at least twenty men, all dressed in black robes, with a small upside down cross with a blue diamond centered over the heart. Dr. Spar snatched the frame out of her hand with a promptness.

"It's not nice to rummage through other people's things!" He shouted.

"Dr. Spar, do not raise your voice at me." She said. He began to liberally sweat, and his word began to slur. "You don't look so good…" She mischievously told him as he fell to his knees and began to pant like a dog in the middle of a Las Vegas summertime heat wave.

"yo…you…you switched the glasses…" He stuttered. Mom stood over him—her heart beating like a drum line—and dug the spike of her high heel into his back and pushed him down to the ground. He looked up at mom through anxious eyes as he slowly began to doze off.

"Well…" Mom began to say before he fully lost consciousness, "…I said I wanted whiskey, not bourbon." Once he was fully out, mom rummaged through her purse for her phone and then called Charles. "I'll be out front in five minutes."

She rummaged through his desk and took a picture of a picture frame with Dr. Spar and Enid Rasp. "Same nose…" She thought to herself. A small, silver key on the desk fit his filing cabinet and she opened the drawers and began to thumb through the many-colored files. She found Tillie, Enzi and Enid Rasp all grouped together in a larger folder title: T.M.M. She grabbed the three files and took them over to the copy machine against the back wall and copied the contents and then stuffed the copies in her purse and returned the files back to their rightful slot, locked the filing cabinet and put the key back in the desk. She cunningly stepped over Dr. Spar as he lay on the floor in a pile of his own drool and grabbed the bronze doorknob until another silent message came from the morning glory: *Get the drug*. She paused at first and then decided to roll Dr. Spar onto his back and search his pockets. Just under the left lapel she found two envelopes full of capsules; one labeled *Heavy-Duty Sleep Sedative* and another envelope just labeled *XXX*.

"He must've grabbed the wrong one by accident." She thought to herself as she took the one marked *XXX* and stuck it in her purse.

She put her ear to the door—the way one would put their ear to the ground—and heard absolutely nothing. No squeaky wheel from a medicine cart, no fanatical screams from the mental patients, just complete and unnatural silence. She gently closed the door behind her as she scurried down the hall towards the exit. She turned around once she was at the double doors as she caught eyes with Tillie.

"Come on…" Charles shouted to mom as she waved at Tillie. Tillie put her finger up to her lips and quickly shooed her away. "Are you okay?" Charles asked as he pushed down on the gas pedal and accelerated quickly, Green Acre's quickly shrinking in the rear-view mirror.

"I will be…we will be." She said and then she mumbled under her breath. "Wherever there is a snake, there is bound to be a charmer…thanks mom."

Chapter Twenty

An hour maybe more had passed by as Tillie and Enzi intolerantly waited in their room for Dr. Spar to declare that they had a visitor.

"What is taking them so long?!" Enzi shouted as she slammed her fists against the decorative pillow that lay on her lap. Tillie rolled her eyes and shook her head, feeling shame. "What is your problem?" Enzi asked. Tillie looked Enzi in her cold eyes—black as a raven—and then rapidly looked down at the herringbone pattern on the floor.

"You seem to be pretty calm. He is about to poison our mother." She said with tremulous hands.

"Good…" Enzi shouted, now standing, towering over Tillie. "…She put us in here…her own daughters." Tillie looked up, unhurriedly; she didn't even recognize her own sister anymore, not even her voice.

"We put us in here. Nobody but us." Tillie sensitively said.

"Whatever. I am going to check on them." Enzi said as Tillie fell back and laid on her back, being hypnotized by the blades of the fan as it spun—counterclockwise—and shook with just the slightest of rattle, a metaphor for her life.

Enzi lightly rapped on Dr. Spar's office door and heard nothing. She slowly jiggled the door handle and was shocked to find that it was unlocked; he was always *very* obstinate about locking doors. She twisted the antiquated door handle and slowly pushed the door open, only to find Dr. Spar lying on the floor on his back, sopping with perspiration.

"Dr. Spar!" Enzi shouted as she rushed to his aid and knelt beside him, dynamically shaking him. "Wake up…please wake up!" She shouted as a passing nurse heard her plea.

"Oh dear, what happened here?" She asked.

"I found him like this." Enzi said.

"I will have to run some tests…" She began to say as she flagged down two orderlies that loaded him onto gurney. "…Straight to the medical wing by care of Dr. Fisher." She instructed as they whisked him away. "Enzi…" The nurse began to gently say as she squeezed a splotch of hand sanitizer into her hand and generously rubbed it into her skin. "…Did you have anything to do with this?" She asked.

"No, I swear. He said that Tillie and I were supposed to have a visitor today and it was taking too long so I came to see what the deal was." Enzi explained. The nurse studied her for a moment.

"Well, I guess patience is not always a virtue. You're a hero. Back to your room now, girl." She said as Enzi nodded and went back to her room.

Mom's hands were still quaking as she sat at my table and cupped both of her hands around a cup of piping hot peppermint tea.

"It calms the nerves…" Charles said as he dropped a sprig of mint leaf into her cup.

"I don't know what this stuff is, mom, but thank God you switched drinks with him." I said as she looked through the twirls of steam which danced off the rim of her cup.

"I don't think that was in my cup. I think he meant to put that in, but he accidentally grabbed a heavy sleep sedative instead." She began to explain. "And what's more, I think that Tillie helped me escape. I saw her and she held her finger up to her lips and then shooed me away, out the door." I looked at her and smiled.

"Well, maybe, when this is all over, there is still hope for Tillie." Mom pressed her lips together and smiled, pleased that I had acknowledged her words.

"Well thank God for the morning glories." Charles happily triumphed.

"Yes…" Mom whispered softly, "…Thank God for the morning glories."

Chapter Twenty-One

A scent had been lingering around the house, hovering in parts that I didn't frequent as often as other areas. A smell of mahogany, chocolate and pipe tobacco. Sometimes it would unpredictably permeate, spontaneously, but it was satisfying none the less.

I walked into the study. It still felt like grandpa's study, and I kept it as it was mostly, only updating the antiquated electrical so that the green Tiffany desk lamp, the one that he got from a trip to New York City, would stop flickering on and off like it was a lightning bug in the strawberry fields.

"Hello." I said as I stepped through the doorway and saw a large lightning bug sitting on the desk, ostensibly peering at me. "Let me get you outside little guy, you shouldn't be alone in here...but thanks for the visit." I said as I laid my hand flat on the desk. The lightning bug crawled onto my hand. I walked outside and stopped in front of the trellis and smiled.

"Here you are…" I said as I held my hand next to the morning glory nearest to the I Love Lucy pendant. I watched as the lightning bug crawled over the closed petals of the bloom and took up space on the pendant, blocking out Lucille Ball's face and replacing it with its euphoric glow. "Have a good day."

I began to turn and go back inside but then a gentle breeze caught my attention and stopped me in my tracks. A familiar soft voice began to whisper in my ears.

"Poodle…thank you…" I looked around and smiled wholly.

"Grandma…hi. Thank me for what?" I asked.

"For bringing my husband to me." She whispered. I was scrupulously puzzled and the look on my face didn't hide the fact that I was.

"Your husband…grandpa?" I asked.

"Yes, silly." She chuckled.

"Can you see him?" I asked. "I guess I assumed that he moved on from this world."

"Poodle, he has been here the whole time, he just hasn't found his voice is all." She said as I contemplated her words. I began to look around as I stopped once my eyes caught sight of the pendant.

"The lightning bugs?" I asked.

"But of course...didn't you hear his song?" She asked. "When one can't find their voice in the Ever After, they find other means of speaking or singing...like the intermittent flickers of light..." She explained as I interrupted.

"Like Morse Code!" I blurted out. She laughed and continued to speak.

"You placed him in my path, I couldn't ask you to do that and he couldn't find it on his own, only you could do this." All the blooms had opened, and they were giving off an alluring smell.

"Because of the magic?" I asked.

"It runs through you. Deep inside your veins like a gold mine. It is in everyone, some..." She began to say as she paused, "...Most people just don't dig deep enough. But it is there, it always has been."

"This just gave me an idea for a song." I said, smiling.

"Well go put it down on paper then, poodle." She happily said.

"I love you. Love you grandpa…you two be good." I said.

"No promises, Poodle, we're going to play hooky." She said as she began to laugh. I laughed, shaking my head and walked inside the house and sat down at the kitchen table and began to play with the words that were flowing out of my fingers, coming out faster than I could write them down. I was onto something: sweet inspiration.

I was still sitting at the table, writing, when Charles walked into the house with Ripp Carnegie.

"See…" Charles began to say, celebrating, "…Just where I said he would be; drinking coffee and writing." Charles finished saying as he slapped me on the back. Ripp smiled as he watched Charles freely move about the kitchen as he found his favorite mug shaped like an owl and another mug for Ripp.

"But *what* is he writing?" Ripp asked as he looked at Charles.

"Something special, probably." Charles said.

"But how do you know?" Ripp asked as I frustratingly put down the pen and let out a long, dramatic and drawn-out sigh.

"Have either of you read the book *Howard's End*?" I asked as they both shook their heads.

"Well, to paraphrase the heroine of E.M. Forster's great novel: *'How do you know what you think until you read what you've written.'*" I said as I looked at Charles and then over at Ripp.

"Like I said, Ripp, something special." Charles said as he poured the coffee into their cups. I looked around the room and smiled deeply. After my conversation with grandma, I was elated.

"You both must be curious as to why I didn't summon you here…" I joked.

"Well, smart ass…" Ripp began to say as he flipped me off, "…*Icky Sticky Sweet Sweet Love* and *Nicest Man You Never Met* have officially entered the charts. Number forty-one and number sixty-seven." Ripp said.

Charles threw his arms around me as Ripp cheered loudly.

"Up and up and up you boys are going." Ripp said as Charles' phone began to vibrate, loudly on the kitchen table. Ripp reached down and grabbed his phone. "It's a text from Nevar." He said as he handed the phone to Charles who anxiously looked at me as I met his gaze. I nodded as he opened his phone. "Well, I just wanted to give you the good news, I have a meeting to get to." Ripp said as he let himself out.

"What did it say?" I asked as Charles looked up from his phone with a baffled look on his face.

"I have to see you, meet me here at 1:00 pm." I read as he handed me the phone.

"They must have found the doctor, it's starting..." I said.

"We better warn your mother." Charles said. "Because I am going to meet her, and I will need you guys to keep eyes on us the whole time." He said.

"We will. Me, mom, grandpa and grandma." I said as he awkwardly raised his eyebrows and cocked his head to the side like a curious dog.

"Your grandpa?" He asked.

"Long story, I'll tell you on the way." I said as we finished our cups of coffee. The smell of tobacco permeated the air exactly where we stood, and I just knew he was near.

Chapter Twenty-Two

"Could you have possibly picked out a more conspicuous outfit?" I asked mom as we followed closely behind Charles in my car as he drove his car to the meeting point; a lonely, cast iron bench in the center of a park overlooking the lake.

"This is a stakeout; you wear black on stakeouts." She smugly stated, clearly, she had seen one too many James Bond films.

"Okay…" I began to say as we made a left turn into the park entrance, "…But what is with the kaleidoscopic garden hat?" I asked. She scoffed and slapped her hand to her chest, mouth agape, clearly offended.

"Oprah wore this hat, Charles…" She scolded as she shook her head, "…OPRAH!" I smiled and rolled down the window as Charles pulled into a parking spot. "Game time!" She sternly said as she unfastened her seatbelt, and I parked the car.

"Mom, what are you doing with that picnic basket?" I asked as Charles began to walk down the paved path into the thicket towards the lake.

"This…" Mom began to say as she liberally shook the basket, "…Has your father's gun in it." She said. Who was this weird and wonderful imposter wearing Oprah's gardening hat, I wondered to myself? Not too long ago she was holding a hand painted glitter sign on the steps of some building in our nation's capital showing her disapproval for the NHRA.

"Well don't shake it!" I said, still shocked that she brought the gun, and that dad gave it to her.

"It's a gun, Charles, not a grenade." She joked as we stopped behind the broad trunk of a mighty oak tree.

Charles sat down on the bench, fretfully chipping away at the paint as it cracked and weakened at the slightest touch. After five minutes, Raven finally arrived and sat down on the bench.

"Hi…" Charles hesitantly said as he slowly looked over at Raven.

"Don't!" She shouted. "Just look forward, watch the ducks or something." His breathing began to quicken, and his palms began to sweat.

"You made it sound important…" He hesitated, "…meeting me here." Raven smiled nervously and casually looked back and forth, like she had a time limit. "Nevar…" He said after a moment of silence. Nothing. "RAVEN!" He shouted as she looked over and caught his eyes. They stared at each other for a moment as Charles began to count the bruises on her face.

"You know?" She asked as her lip quivered. "It doesn't matter anymore. Look at my face…" She said through defeated eyes, "…This is what happens when you fail your first mission." She said. "You guys don't know what you are up against, they are everywhere." Charles slowly crawled his hand over and rested it on top of her hand.

"Who did this to you?" He asked as she quickly pulled her hand away.

"People that you may or may not know; Enid Rasp and Enzi Ponder. They used a burlap sack full of apples from the orchard." She explained as she pulled out one of the apples from her purse. "I'm supposed to give this to you. *They* gave it to me to give to you…" She said as she held the apple up in the air, as if to study it under the rays of the sun. "…It was poisoned, but I switched it." She said. Charles looked at her and then frantically looked around, planning an exit strategy if needed, or possibly he was looking for Oprah's hat. "I have done nothing but lie to you, but I promise I switched the apple. I need you to take a bite of it right now, please." She pleaded as he sat there holding the apple.

"And why should I trust you now?" He asked.

"Because they are watching, and if you don't, they will kill you and me." She said. Charles studied her eyes; they were full of fear and trepidation. Either she just gave an Oscar worthy performance, or she was telling the truth. He must have thought it was the latter as he took a bite of the apple. "Thank you. Tell Charles that I am sorry and that it's not too late to get Tillie back. Enzi belongs to them now. They are going to attack very soon, be ready." She began to explain as her breathing quickened.

"What about you?" Charles asked.

"They think you ate the poisoned apple. That bought me two days of silence. I bought a one-way ticket to stay with a relative who lives in Canada, I'm leaving tonight." She said as she stood up to leave. She walked behind the bench as Charles looked forward.

"Something is happening…" I said as mom stuck her hand in the picnic basket and wrapped her hand around the pistol grip.

"A Mystic Mile brother has been tampering with your vehicle, don't drive it." Raven said as she quickly walked down the path, out of sight from Charles. As she got down the path, she glanced to her right and accidentally crossed paths with mom and me.
"Charles…Evonne…you should *not* be here." She said as she stared at me, ashamed. "Don't let Charles drive his vehicle. They likely didn't know your vehicle was here, take yours." She said as she began to walk away.

"Raven!" Mom shouted as Raven stopped and slowly turned to face her. "Life doesn't get better by chance; it gets better by change." She said as Raven slightly smiled and left.

We got to the vehicle which was parked across the parking lot from Charles' and we cautiously watched everyone who passed by.

"Anyone could be in The Mystic Mile, so watch *everyone*." Mom said as I obeyed, waiting for Charles to come out of the thicket. He took a different path, armed only with a Swiss Army Knife that he had in his front pocket. "There he is!" Mom shouted as she flagged him down before he got to his vehicle. He heard the shouts coming from the rented vehicle that we sat in and he ran to where we were.

"DRIVE! He shouted as he jumped in the vehicle. I put it in drive, reversed and quickly accelerated away.

"Your vehicle..." I began to say as he interrupted me.

"Was tampered with. I know, Raven warned me. She is running away from them. Enzi and Enid Rasp were forced to beat her with a bag full of solid apples. She said that Enzi belongs to them, but Tillie can still be saved." He said as moms' eyes glossed over.

"See, Charles, we can at least save her. I knew she helped me." Mom said, completely overjoyed.

"You were right, mom, we will try everything we can to get her! Let's just get out of here." I said as Charles pulled out his phone and began to dial. "Who are you calling?" I asked.

"The police...I am reporting my car as stolen." Charles said.

"What are you going to tell them, that these crazy cult people stole it?" I asked.

"I am going to say that a few days ago someone put a note on my car saying that they were going to cut my brakes if I didn't leave the keys under the front right tire. They will just tow it and do a full inspection when it gets to the impound lot." He said as the 911 operator answered the phone and he began to explain everything.

"This is almost over." Mom said as she reached over and squeezed my hand. "I can feel it."

Chapter Twenty-Three

Three days it had been since the morning glories had last rested their somnolent petals as they kept an attentive stem out for trouble, all day and all night. You could sense it in the atmosphere, something was awry.

The foxes had stopped cavorting; the deer had stopped grazing and the birds had stopped flying overhead. Another part of what made this place so magical was their presence, but in their absence, something alternatively magical had begun to happen. Grandma and grandpa had contacted others from the Ever After. Others who had roamed the Earth trying to be remembered and asked them to inhabit the surrounding trees and forests around the farm; the ultimate surrender just to be remembered.

"Grandma, who are they?" I asked when I began to hear the lively chatter and the singing.

"They are the forgotten, poodle. Pilgrims; aristocrats, poets, politicians, murderers and singers." She happily said; delighted to be able to commune.

"How many are there?" I asked.

"Right now I have seventy-six, thirteen of which have yet to find their voices." She said. "I promised all of the that they would always be remembered on this land, Poodle, it will be up to you to get to know each and every one of them…and in return they will always protect you, this place, and they will always keep the magic alive." I smiled as I looked out at the vacant strawberry fields which were full of repartee. I could see no one, but I could hear and fell all of them.

"Deal, grandma, I will know all of them. Thank you all." I appreciatively praised as the wind blew cordiality through my thick locks.

I walked inside the house and sat down in the kitchen at the table and began to draft a text message to mom, Charles and dad. *Dinner tonight at my place, 6:30, don't be late.* I pushed send and, as I waited for a response, a beautiful, brilliant crimson ladybug crawled across the table. "Hello…" I said as it stopped crawling and turned to face me. It appeared to be studying me as we just stared, languidly, at each other. "…Have you not found your voice yet?" I asked after a moment of stillness had elapsed.

"No…I mean yes, I have found my voice…" She said, timidly. "…My apologies. I had forgotten what it is like to be spoken to." She finished saying as I smiled. I stuck my finger in front of her as she crawled onto my fingertip and I brought her up to my eye level to see her better.

"How long as it been, ma'am?" I asked. "I'm Charles, by the way."

"Antoinette Denos," She began to say, "And I died in 1910." I stared sorrowfully at her. This soul that has inhabited the body of this ladybug that was strikingly red. I could feel her pain and her happiness swirling around in the air like the funnel cloud before the tornado.

"Well, Antoinette, I will help you find your descendants…if you like." I offered. I could feel her smiling. "There are a lot of you out there, but I promise to get to all of you." I said.

"No rush. In time you will meet all of us. But for now I am only glad to be talking to someone other than myself. I am going to check the land." She said as she fluttered her petite wings and flew out the kitchen window. I grabbed my pen and scribbled into my notebook: *Antoinette, ladybug, 1910*, just as my phone dinged.

"We'll be there." Mom responded.

"I'll bring the wine." Charles responded.

I smiled as I closed the text message thread and brought up the internet and began to Google who Antoinette Denos from 1910 was and began to do my research on her history.

Antoinette Denos was born in 1850 and died in 1910. She was a socialite whose father was the president of a conglomerate outside of Buffalo, New York. He made his money in in steel and, upon his untimely death of being crushed by a steel beam that fell from above, his final will in testament was to leave everything to his only daughter Antoinette. She later married Benjamin Denos and they had their five children: three boys and two girls. When Antoinette died in 1910, she was preceded in death by her only surviving child, her daughter Abigail. Abigail was born April 1, 1888 and died July 3, 1992 at the elderly age of one hundred and five years old, surrounded by her children, grandchildren and great grandchildren.

"This is where I will start, with Abigail's children." I said as I took note of all the pertinent information that I could find. I didn't care if I had to research every single soul that was floating around outside, I would talk to every tree, bush and bug until I honored grandmas request and helped them all become remembered and stay remembered.

Chapter Twenty-Four

It was easy enough to convince mom to tell Sean, Travis and their families to take an all-expenses paid—by me—trip away from here for the next two weeks. I found an all-inclusive resort for families in Hawaii, on the big island, and they were set to board their departing plane any time now.

"Mom stop crying… Sean said as he hugged her, "…We will only be gone two weeks. I had a lot of PTO anyways."

I understood why she was so expressive. Hell, for all we knew, The Mystic Mile had resources we were unaware of. Although nothing could weigh against the magic and the horde of The Remembered—which now inhabited everything around here. The Mystic Mile were capable of something far more menacing and precarious than anything we had, the dark side of the heart. There is a lot of danger in the darkness, but somehow the light always gets in and, even more furtively, always prevails.

"Okay mom, it's time to call. Let's see what happens." I said as I handed her the phone as it rang. She gave me a disconcerted look as she grabbed the phone.

"This is Dr. Spar; how may I help you?" He said as he answered the phone. The baritone in his tone of voice sent shivers down moms' spine as she slightly cringed.

"Hello Dr. Spar, its Evonne Ponder…I was wondering how the girls are doing?" She asked as congenially as she could muster. Dr. Spar chuckled lightly.

"You have got some balls; I will give you that…" he began to say boldly. "…You do not need to worry yourself about Tillie and Enzi. Not anymore. They belong to me now…their *real* family." He said. Mom began to get irate as she got a sudden glazed look in her eyes.

"They are not! They are MINE!" She shouted.

"Don't believe me? Ask them for yourself…" He smugly said. "…Enzi, talk to your mother." S moment of silence fell over both ends of the phone as the click of Enzi's heels struck the hard wood flooring as she walked across the office closer to the phone, sounding like a Clydesdale.

"You shouldn't have tried to kill him, mother. He loves me and has selected me to be his bride." Enzi happily said. "And just you wait, we're coming for you. We're coming for all of you!" She shouted.

"Tillie…" Dr. Spar began to demand, "…Tell her." Tillie undecidedly walked over to the phone and leaned over the receiver.

"Uhm…hi mom…" She softly began to speak. "…Where is Raven?" She asked.

"Tell her that Raven is dead." I softly whispered into moms' ear as I brushed her auburn hair—the color of fall—behind it.

"Raven is dead." Mom said.

"Hmm, lucky her." Tillie uncaringly said as Enzi swiftly pushed her face away from the phone.

"Get her out of here now. I will deal with her attitude later!" Dr. Spar said as Enzi escorted Tillie back to their room. Enid, finish this." He said as he stormed out of the room.

"Enid Rasp…" Mom began to say in her recognizable, compassionate motherly tone, "…Your father doesn't have to do this. You don't have to do this." Enid Rasp began to laugh manically.

"The next step of enlightenment for all of us is only reached when your hearts all stop beating. When the last drop of blood leaves your body." She said. "So, as you can see, we *do* have to do this…in three days' time. We're coming for you. All of you!" She said as she slammed the phone down onto the receiver. Mom stood there, trembling, as she looked around the room.

"Mom…" I began to say as she held up her hand, stopping me from speaking.

"Whatever happens, promise that you will try to get Tillie. Her voice was normal…but Enzi, well, she is gone." Mom began to say as I walked over to her and put my arms around her shoulders.

"Dad, how much ammo can we buy without looking suspicious." I asked.

"No…" Mom sternly said. "…This is not a fight that will require guns and ammo; we need your grandma, grandpa and all of The Remembered." I nodded as I agreed with her.

"Charles, now might be the perfect time for you to take a vacation." I said as he looked at me crossly.

"I have been through too much already. I am *way* too involved. Besides…I love you…all." He said, as he corrected himself.

"He is right, Charles." Mom said as she reached her hand up and rubbed mine as it rested on her shoulder. "Charles is in this whether he wants to be or not. She told us: three days from now. That was the only warning we will get. Now we have one hundred and nineteen acres of magic surround this place. If we plan this right, we will know their every step." Mom said.

"Breakfast tomorrow at our house, we will start to plan." Dad suddenly said as he looked around the room.

"Okay…well you all should take off before the sun burns out." I said as I looked over at Charles just as he caught my gaze and gave me a challenging stare.

"Don't even think about it. I am staying here with you." He said. It would have been a futile effort to argue with him; after all, he was right. He was entirely too involved, and he had seen things…unexplainable things that nobody could possibly understand.

Who better to help us than him?

Chapter Twenty-Five

Charles and I sat in an office next to the new studio with Ripp Carnegie and one of his bosses. The irresistible smell of rich mahogany and coriander enhanced the opulence of his office.

"Stu, I want you to officially meet Charles and Charles." Ripp said as he introduced us to his boss. Ripp's boss, Stuart Blaze, was an amazingly comfortable man who made an even more comfortable living. He had not an ounce of fat on his body and looked like the type of prosperous, affluent man whose idea of lunch would be to suck diet coke out of a sopping cotton ball. I could almost hear his stomach petitioning someone, anyone, to tie him down to a chair and force a cheeseburger down his throat. Stuart was the type of man in the magazines, sitting in the Top Ten of the *World's Most Beautiful Men*. As he spoke, affably, with Charles, I studied him closely. What it must be like to be so stunning, so inhumanly faultless, that you will never be good enough for yourself and you will always be riddled with dysmorphia of some kind. I wanted to hug him and comfort him.

"It's okay…" I would tell him, "…Of all the bad things I have been through and all the bad things I am currently going through…I feel for you. Hell, I might be dead in two days, but it's you, sir, that I feel bad for. So here is a Snickers candy bar." I thought to myself as Ripp shook my arm and I snapped out of my gauche staring contest with Stu. "I'm sorry, what?" I asked.

"I asked why your music and your songs are so damn good." Stu said. I looked around the office as I caught eyes with Charles; he gave me a nod as I carefully thought of my response.

"Well, Stu, because my…" I paused as Charles cleared his throat, "…I mean *our* music loves us as much as we love it." Ripp smiled; clearly, he was very satisfied with my answer.

"How elegiac and keen, so what brings you all to the big city?" He asked. I couldn't exactly tell him that Charles and I were meeting with a woman whom mom met online; a woman who *used* to be a member of The Mystic Mile but had escaped from their clutches—like Raven did—so that we can pick her brain and be ready for whatever they have in store for us.

"Inspiration." I convincingly lied.

"I'm sorry, what was that?" Stu asked as Ripp gave me a puzzling look. I walked over to the window, unlatched it and opened it.

"Inspiration." I repeated. "What is New York if not a giant symphony without an interlude? The fuss from the pigeons, the blinkers from the taxis, the squeaky wheel from the hot dog vendor. It is all music in its own form; it is just up to us if we allow ourselves to hear it as such or not." I said.

"Charles, you have a beautiful way of looking at life." Stu said. "Ripp, I see what you see in him…I mean in *them*." He said as Ripp walked over and put his arms around my shoulders. "And you, Charles…" Stu began to say as he shifted his gaze, "…With your voice, you two are unstoppable." We all looked at each other and smiled graciously. "I had initially set a meeting for the end of next week to possibly renegotiate and negotiate your contracts…" He said as he paused and walked over to the other window and opened it, letting New York City roam around the room. "I'm sure we can easily accommodate. Ripp, whatever they want, within reason, present it to me next week. I have seen what I need to see." He said as he looked at Charles and me and then walked over to his office door and opened it, motioning for us to leave. On my way out of the office Stu grabbed my arm. "Thank you" He said as his flawless smile brightened the room. "It has been more than fifteen years since those old windows have opened." I smiled and walked out; my head held a little higher than normal.

For all the negative things that have been happening…" Charles began to say as we sat in the cab on our way to meet the ex-Mystic Mile member, "…Today was nice. I Feel reenergized." He said.

"Me too!" I said.

"How did you find this contact anyways?" He asked.

"Mom found her on a forum online when she was trying to understand more about The Mystic Mile." I said as the taxi slowed to a stop. "Put your phone in airplane mode and record the conversation." I said as he nodded his head in abeyance.

I stepped out of the taxi. The slight thud from the door shutting made me remember the night the cops arrested Raven, Enzi and Tillie; I cringed then too. The air seemed substantial here, almost like an admonition. Only this time, Charles felt it too.

"Are we sure about this?" He asked. "I mean we are going in there unarmed and unaware." I looked up towards the sky and he followed suit.

"Antoinette Denos." I shouted. I held my hand up in the air and, after a few moments, a strikingly red ladybug landed on my palm. "We're not alone, Charles. Are we Antoinette?" I asked as the wind carried a soft whisper.

"Never alone with us." She said as Charles' eyes widened in astonishment.

"Let's go." I said as I opened the door. The bell chimed, announcing us as I greeted the lady at the counter as Charles slid a rock in the door frame, keeping it from closing all the way. "We're here to see Marla." I said as she pointed towards a doorway draped in heavy wooden beads.

"She is expecting you." The front desk associate announced.

We sat down in matching chairs which were clad in green velvet, around a table with a crystal ball in the center of it. The walls were heavily clad in deep, royal purple velvet which added to the mysteriousness of the atmosphere. We sat in silence for a few moments until a faint chanting type of music began to lightly play. She entered the room, Marla did, and sat in the vacant chair across from us. I was taken back at how vapid she appeared to be. Nothing about her screamed out mystic or mysterious. Her uninteresting, dreary flaxen hair and economical lipstick left no traces of anything memorable.

"Marla Pereaux." She mystically said as she acknowledged Charles and me.

"We come for answers." I began to say as she dragged her finger across her lips.

"I know why you've come. Evonne Ponder paid me to answer questions for you, but only three." She instructed. "What is your first question?" She asked. I thought for a while before speaking.

"Is it too late to get my sisters back?" I asked.

"I have seen this all already; Tillie can be reached but Enzi is no more. She is to be wed." She said as she peered deeply into the crystal ball. "What is your next question?" I looked at Charles and he met my gaze and smiled lightly.

"How many people are in The Mystic Mile?" He asked. Marla reached for the thick golden ring on her middle finger and turned it upside down and struck the ruby on the top of the crystal ball. We watched, in amazement, as the crystal ball began to spin.

"What you are dealing with is just a single chapter in a larger fraternal order. The Mystic Mile reaches all shores. Even if you win, you will lose in the end." She coldly stated, sounding more and more like one of the few active members we have encountered.

"Well they have no idea what I am capable of…" I said as I looked over at Charles and smiled.

"What *we're* capable of…" Charles said. Marla silently nodded and creased a smile that revealed everything; years of panic and running, and years of looking over her shoulder.

"What is your final question?" She asked.

"My…*our* final question must be this: Marla, as someone who has fought this fight before, what are we up against?" I asked as I reached out and tapped the crystal ball. It stopped spinning and abruptly began to freely float in midair.

"It's levitating…" Marla said, astonished, as she looked at me even deeper than before.

"Could you please answer the question?" I brusquely asked.

"Of course…" She said as she cleared her throat. She was still clearly taken aback by the floating crystal ball. "The Mystic Mile is nothing more than a fraternal order of men who believe they have a gift. There is absolutely nothing *mystic* about them. What I witnessed with the crystal ball was something mystic. They have people in high places…they have connections…but they don't have what you have. You may just defeat them after all. Now it is time for you both to leave. At this moment I sense they are planning something big. Best of luck." She said as her lip quivered and she got up and left the room.

"Let's get out of here Charles." I said as we got up and left the velvet room. I stopped at the front counter. "Ma'am, can I have a piece of paper and a pen?" I asked as she honored my request.

"What are you doing?" Charles asked.

"I just want to leave Marla a small note." I began to say as I wrote down the message. I handed it to Charles, and he read it out loud.

"Marla, once all of this is over, I will tell you so that you can finally live in peace. That is my promise to you."

Chapter Twenty-Six

Time seemed to unnervingly tick by slowly. Hour's felt like days and days felt like weeks. I had vowed to live my life to its fullest and find something in every single day worth smiling for and appreciating whole heartedly, but why did I vow this mere days before what may just be the biggest fight of my life? I sat by my bedroom window as a gentle breeze rolled in and danced around the room. The saccharine smell of strawberries and lavender reminded me of the past. Of less convoluted times. The window was now bordered with morning glories of all colors and hues, profound purple and brilliant blue, fantastic fuchsia and inconceivable indigo. There was even an emblazoned red orange which came to exist shortly after I brought grandpa back to grandma.

"This is the color of a heart that has been jump started." Grandma told me when I enquired about the other worldly dye that was now completing the rainbow of morning glories which were now stretched to all one hundred and nineteen magical acres surround the house.

I had been waiting—rather impatiently—for creativity to strike me once more as I sat in my chair next to the window with a pen in hand and pad of paper resting on my lap. One simple sentence hit me like a bolt of lightning: *Tell me what you see when you look into my eyes, stare at a puddle of water until it dries.* I hadn't the slightest clue of what to do with these words. I knew it was to be used in song that I had not written yet. NO, that would come to me later, most likely at the most inconvenient time. But creativity has no schema or schedule, it just simply floats around waiting for an artistic soul to open and be receptive. That could happen anytime and anyplace. We can't burden creativity for doing her job.

"Grandma..." I softly began to croon as one of the deep mauve morning glories—the color of midnight strolls next to a rivers edge—turned to face me. "What is with the myriad of colors?" I asked.

"Eudaimonia..." She retorted.

"You have pneumonia? How can a soul inhabiting a flower get pneumonia?" I asked, slightly concerned. She began to laugh. Light chuckles at first but then they grew louder and deeper. Antoinette

Denos was laughing, grandpa was laughing, hell, all The Remembered were laughing.

"No, silly boy…" Grandma said, still slightly amused. "Eudaimonia is the highest degree of happiness that one can achieve…read a book once in a while, Poodle!" She explained as she began to chortle once more.

"Hmm, the highest degree of happiness you say?" I said as I pondered her words. We were on the precipice of some type of war with a sect that reached every shore, how could I be happy at this time? "Grandma, how can I focus on eudaimonia with all the crap that I…" I paused and exhaled, "…that we are dealing with?" I asked. She sighed as a draft of annoyance blew in the room.

"Poodle, if you argue for your imitations, then you get to keep them." She scolded. I sat back in the chair as I twirled the stem of the morning glory between my thumb and index finger.

"You are absolutely right. I don't know what I was thinking…thank you." I appreciatively said.

"You are all facing a lot right now. The other day your mother was in the park talking to a tree, thinking it was me." She said as she began to laugh.

"Did you answer her?" I asked. Somehow, I knew the answer was going to be in line with her absurdity.

"Absolutely not! She looked too funny talking to a tree." She said as she laughed.

"I'll never understand your sardonic humor, grandma, but I am glad that I have you." I said as Antoinette flew in the window.

"Charles, the first members have posted in the thicket. There are three of them." She said as I looked at the morning glory.

"Keep a watchful eye, Antoinette." I said as I cleared my throat. I sent the emergency text code to mom, dad and Charles. *Have you spoken to the Morning Glories?* "Grandma…" I said as I held the morning glory up to my face, eye level.

"It has begun, Poodle…" She circumspectly said as the barrage of flowers faced outward in every direction, taking up siege.

Chapter Twenty-Seven

Nothing ever happens the way that you suppose it will. You replay situations over and over inside of your head of how you perceive it will happen, and then, a wrench. A striking, burnished, unanticipated wrench.

"So, there is something special about him?" Dr. Spar said as he circled the chair that an unknown person was bounded too. They had been brought in by other members of The Mystic Mile.

"Do you know who I am?" She asked from behind the burlap sack that muffled her breathing and her voice.

"I have an idea…" He said as he dragged his index finger across her chest, tracing her clavicle. She shuttered at his touch and shook her head in a defiant manner.

"We found her after Charles and his friend left her shop. She was sitting at the front counter." One of the brothers of The Mystic Mile gloated.

"Well done…" Dr. Spar praised. "Now go and meet up with the others at the edge of the woods, it is almost time." He said as they left. "Now, what to do with you?" He asked as he examined the chair bindings. "Are these too tight?"

"Yes, my hands and fingers are numb. She said. The burlap sack was splashed with wet patches, silent sobs of fear.

"I have more questions. How you answer then depends on how well you get treated, understood?" He asked.

"LET ME GO! YOU CAN'T DO THIS!" She screamed. Her once silent sobs of fright had evolved into bawling like that of a five-year-old in the cereal aisle of a supermarket.

"I love it when they scream and cry." Dr. Spar said as he looked over at Tillie who stood in the corner, frightened herself, but too afraid to show how she really felt.

"Leave us, Tillie!" He demanded.

"Now why would Charles seek out the help from a psychic? A lonely, pathetic psychic with nothing and nobody?" He asked as he belittled her. She was silent as she attempted to manage another eruption of tears and screams.

"Hello…" He said loudly as he tightened the straps on her wrists. She let out a whimper but still refused to speak. "ANSWER ME!" He shouted as he ripped the burlap sack off her head. He walked over to the lamp and removed the shade. Suddenly the room flooded with light. Dr. Spar went silent, his hand covering his mouth. He took a step back, and then another, and then another until his back was flat against the cold, damp concrete wall. Marla Pereaux slowly lifted her head. Her hair parted just enough for Dr. Spar to recognize her plain eyes which were only recognizable to him.

"Marla, how…how can this be?" He asked. He was still stunned, as if he had seen a ghost. She looked at him, hurt and defeat plastered across her face.

"You are the reason that I left. It all became too much for me and not enough for you." She sobbed.

"Too much for you" He fired back. "I loved you! I never stopped!" He shouted even louder.

"Well, you have a funny way of showing it." She screamed, matching his decibel. "And if you're wondering about Charles…" She softly said as his ears perked up, "…He is special. You will not win this one." He looked at her suddenly full of remorse—years of remorse—as he stumbled to the chair that Marla was bound to and began to unshackle her wrist bindings. She vigorously rubbed her pained wrists as she glared at him.

"Can you ever forgive me, Marla?" He asked. This was the man that she fell for all those years ago who drug her heart through the mud in the worst of ways, and now he wanted forgiveness? This was the man who, as of recent, tried to kill my mother and now plans to marry my little sister, and now he wants pity? Suddenly, Marla realized that she held the upper hand, maybe for the first time in her life.

"Let me go…" She sniffled. "…Let me go and I will *consider* forgiving you." She finished saying as she studied his sodden eyes.

"We're in the middle of a dense forest, it's dangerous out there. Let me at least drive you to the nearest town." He suggested.

"I'll take my chances in the forest." She derisively said, suddenly holding *all* the cards.

"Very well, you are free to go." He said as he turned around to face the wall. Marla bolted out the door, up the stairs and into the thickness of the forest.

Ridley Biggs, a man who died in an avalanche in the sixties, had inhabited the mighty oak trees that filled the forests around the house. He unexpectedly shouted over the air.

"Charles! A woman in the thicket…she is running scared!" I looked over at Charles and then over at mom as her eyes suddenly lit up.

"Tillie! Maybe it's Tillie!" Mom shouted.

"Ridley, clear a path and send her here." I hollered.

Marla ran as fast as she could through the thicket, breathing heavily and crying as she tripped over the root of a tree. She lay there; catching her breath as she unexpectedly looked up to the sound of the cracking and creaking of the tree branches overhead, bending. One by one, the branches began to point in the direction that would lead her to safety. She stared in awe as the path became more and more clear. She hadn't felt this sort of serene since the day the crystal ball levitated. She understood immediately that she was safe with the trees as she sprinted through the coppice and into the clear open strawberry fields. Mom stood at the fence line—the same fence line where we found grandpa—hoping that it would be Tillie.

"Help me! Please help me!" Marla shouted as she ran towards mom. Mom didn't recognize her as she turned and ran back into the house, but I did recognize her and her voice as I ran to the fence line. Marla instantaneously recognized me and, for the first time in years, felt wholly and unreservedly safe as she fainted and collapsed. Her head landed softly, cradled in a pile of morning glories.

"Get her inside, Charles." Grandma said as Antoinette Denos landed on the fence post.

"Charles, two more have posted at the edge of the forest." I thanked her and carried Marla into the safety of the house.

Chapter Twenty-Eight

"Instead of crying, just keep on trying. Don't waste a failure."

Grandma quietly whispered that to Marla as she aggressively thrashed in her sleep, getting more and more wrapped in the bed sheets. She awoke hurriedly; sweat beading off her forehead as she glanced around the room.

"Who...who said that?" She cautiously asked as she continued to look around the room.

"I did." Grandma whispered.

"Where are you? Was I drugged?" She asked, now more interested and less cautious.

"Down here dear girl..." Grandma said. Marla looked down to see a prolific purple morning glory resting in her lap. Marla studied the bloom for a moment and then brought the amethyst up to her nose, inhaling deeply.

"I'm safe here, aren't I?" Marla asked as she twirled the flower between her fingers by the stem and then slid it behind her ear.

"You are." Grandma said just as mom walked into the bedroom with a tray that had freshly baked blueberry muffins and freshly squeezed orange juice.

"You must be famished…" Mom began to say as she offered her some indulgence. "Don't worry; we're here to help you." Marla looked at her through unadorned eyes as they began to overflow once more with tears.

"I thought I had escaped all of this. I really thought that I was hiding in plain sight." She began to confess as mom sat next to her. "But then I got abducted in the middle of broad daylight. I screamed for help, but it was New York City, everyone just looked the other way." Mom began to run her fingers through Marla's hair as it calmed her rapid heartbeat.

"Do you know who took you?" Mom asked as she readjusted the morning glory in Marla's ear.

"Two men, one had red hair. But it was Billy Spar who was behind it. No doubt he orchestrated the whole thing." She complained.

"Billy…" Mom began to think out loud, suddenly realizing that she never actually knew his first name. "Dr. Spar has my two daughters…" Mom began to confess. "…He tried to poison me not too long ago. Anyways…" Mom continued as she shook those agonizing memories away, "…I hope it's not too late for my girls." Marla reached up and grabbed moms' hand, mid brush stroke, and looked her in the eyes.

"Where I was being held…on the edge on the forest in a concrete bunker…Tillie was there. Billy yelled at her to leave. He didn't want her to see the sick, wicked things he was going to do to me." Marla said.

"What did he do to you?" Mom asked, slightly disturbed.

"Nothing, he took the bag off my head and was surprised to see that it was me." Marla explained as mom mentally took notes. "You see, Billy and I…years ago…were happily engaged. We met in college. But he also met some other people who introduced him to a better way of life. It was harmless at first, the parties…the money…the profligacy of it all. But then they demanded more and more, and he slowly slipped under their spell." She said as she looked at mom, "That's how they get you." Tears were beginning to well up in her eyes once again as she sniffed them away. "Now he has become this monster. I have seen all this far too many times; Enzi has made up her mind. But Tillie, she is beginning to get restless. You can still get her. I can help you." Marla said.

"Please! That is all I want, for all of this to be over and to have my Tillie back in my arms." Mom said.

"Are we sure that this place is safe? They are everywhere." Marla said.

"This place is safe. It's magical. There are spirits who inhabit the grounds around here. My mom…" She said as she gently plucked the morning glory from behind Marla's ear and held it up in the air.

"Is that who spoke to me?" Marla asked. Her eyes, life-sized like that day that the crystal ball levitated.

"It was me, dear sweet girl." Grandma said, her syrupy words rolling off the petals in the form of the sweetest aroma.

"Ma'am…" Marla began to softly ask, "…What did you mean when you said, 'instead of crying just keep on trying'?" She looked at mom, who cut her a sliver of a smile. For most of Marla Pereaux's adult life, she has had to look over her shoulders in fear.

"I can see and feel all of your hardships, and, although you have been through more than the average person, you are letting it define you." Grandma explained. "You are strong, beautiful and you truly have a gift. Otherwise you wouldn't hear me." Marla's tensed shoulders relaxed as she exhaled.

"In with the good, out with the bad." Mom said as she tied a red ribbon—the color of new beginnings—in her hair, pulling it out of her face, revealing two sapphires. Two dazzling sapphires that had been hidden behind years of angst. "There you are…the real you." Mom said, smiling.

I stood at the kitchen sink; the light reflected off the copper sink as it streaked a strobe of warmth across my cheek. Antoinette Denos flew in and landed on the windowsill.

"Ma'am…" I nodded, acknowledging her presence. "Any update?" I asked.

"Just more men at the edge of the forest, camped out. Not quite on our land." She jubilantly said, glad to be here and helping all of us.

"…How many men are there?" I asked.

"I have counted forty-five. I heard one say they were awaiting the final two and then they would be given the order to proceed." She said. I peered out the window just as a gust of wind danced in the open strawberry fields. It was so peaceful and serene, like a mid-daydream.

"Two more would put them at forty-seven…" I began to ponder out loud. "…With the seventy-six of you all, and the forty-seven of them…that makes one hundred and twenty-three. Odd…" I thought.

"What is it Charles?" Antoinette asked. I looked at her and smiled.

"Maybe nothing, maybe something. Could you alert all of The Remembered and tell them to be ready…and to expect anything." I asked as she flew off into the balmy, cerulean sky.

Mom and Marla Pereaux walked into the kitchen; grandma tucked snugly behind Marla's ear. I stared in awe; I was taken aback by Marla's beauty.

"This must be what it looks like to completely let go of all that you cannot change." I thought to myself. "Marla, I hope that you are feeling better. Something big will be happening here, soon. If you would like to leave, you can take my car." I suggested. She smiled as she adjusted the bloom in her ear and smiled at mom.

"Thanks Charles, but I can actually be of some help to you." She said as she looked out the window. "To all of you."

Chapter Twenty-Nine

"Mom, can I ask you a question?" I asked as I Sat at the table with my hands cupped around my freshly brewed coffee, the color of russets.

"Of course, Charles, what's on your mind?" She asked. I looked at her, thinking about my question—silence. I opened my mouth, but nothing came out. My lips couldn't form the words. "Charles…" She softly said as she sauntered across the kitchen and sat next to me, rubbing my arm. Charles stood by the window, staring at me. "Whatever it is, Charles, you can ask." She said.

"Mom, when I was little and refused to go to sleep…" I began to say as I looked at her, "What was the excuse that I gave you?" I asked. From the age of ten all the way up until I was fifteen, I did everything I possibly could to not go to sleep.

"Nightmares, you told me." She said. I frowned as I looked her in the eyes and then down at the floor. "What is this about, Charles?"

"I lied to you, mom." I told her, ashamed that I had carried this baggage. This weight around with me for so long.

"Lied about what…the nightmares?" She asked. I nodded my head.

"When I was ten years old, you made me go to my old bus drivers' funeral…" I began to explain, "…Do you remember?" I asked.

"Connie Jane? Of course I do." She said.

"When I looked at her, she looked like she was stuck in a state of sleep, like Cinderella or Snow White. I didn't understand the difference between sleep and death. They looked the same to me." I told her. Charles came and sat by me, wholly fascinated by my outlook that I had and curious about where this exchange was going. "It wasn't until I was fifteen that I finally understood death."

"Why are you telling me all of this now? It's been over fifteen years." She said, inquisitively. I smirked as I looked at Charles. Why did I trust him so much? Why was I so comfortable around him?

"I guess when it gets close to the end; you start to think about the beginning." I told her. She smiled as she squeezed my arm.

"Well son, every ending is just another beginning." She poetically said as Antoinette Denos fluttered in the window.

"We have been calling out to you, have you not been hearing us?" She asked, gallingly. We all went silent as Ridley Biggs began to bay over the treetops.

"ITS HAPPENING!" He shouted.

I looked at mom as she looked over at Marla Pereaux who then looked over at Charles who then looked over at me...I shifted my gaze to Antoinette.

"Charles, the final two have arrived and the order has been given." She alertly explained. My inhalation began to accelerate, and my heart began to echo like the pitter patter of the swollen rain drops on the windshield on that dreadful day on the bridge, the look in Enzi's eyes as she rammed our vehicle over and over, pushing us closer and closer to the edge of the cold, mossy rock wall, the river roaring in anticipation of our unpredicted advent.

"Antoinette, Ridley, Grandpa, everyone...just as we planned. The moment you see Tillie, separate her. Lead her down a different path." I began to firmly speak as my words were carried by the wind to all stretches of the one hundred and nineteen magical acres. "Remember, do NOT underestimate The Mystic Mile, they have resources, but they do not have all of you." I began to remind them all as an unfamiliar voice began speaking directly to me.

"I apologize for the intrusion, but I have found my voice." He said as his words were conveyed with a substantial, British brogue.

"Who are you?" I asked.

"Chester Potts, sir." He said.

"Chester, glad to have you with us…" I began to say as Charles— who had been typing away on his cell phone—flashed his screen at me. I read for a moment a brief narrative about a Chester Potts from London. "Chester Potts? Like the English privateer from the 1700's Chester Potts?" I asked.

"Aye, that is me." He said.

"You were known as the Prince of the English Channel…" I said.

"That was me, sir…" He said.

"Well, welcome. What have you become?" I asked.

"The ground. I am all the dirt, soil and all the rocks." He said. I smiled as I looked at grandma who had bloomed near the open window.

"Hmm, he can be of some *very* good use." Grandma said.

"Chester don't be afraid to dig deep holes and trap them inside. Remember, everyone, their intention may be to harm us…maybe even kill us. But that is not who we are. Trap them, cut off their resources and even shake them up a little bit. Trust me, they will retreat." I said.

"How can you be so sure?" Marla Pereaux asked just as dad walked into the kitchen. A flash of light reflected off his polished handgun that was resting on his hip.

"People who believe in superstitions become superstitious themselves." I said, self-assuredly.

I looked around the room, getting a good look at everyone and remembering just how each of their journeys had led them to this exact moment. A sudden gust of brisk wind blew in through the kitchen window and danced around the room. The burning sun began to lower its curtain and the moon was on the rise as grandpa and his horde of fireflies began to fleck the fields and the night sky, replacing the twinkling stars. Grandma stretched her vines and bloomed her night petals in all directions, covering the house with her shielding aroma. And Antoinette Denos—the voice of all the ladybugs—collected her masses from near and far and unwearyingly waited in the strawberry fields, becoming the strawberry fields.

"It's like a sea of Crimson…" I thought to myself as I peered out the window. Ridley Biggs stretched out his branches and interweaved them together, creating a near impenetrable wall of prickly branches, leaving only three direct paths to the house. Chester would be waiting to separate all but three: Dr. Spar, Enzi and Enid Rasp, who would be granted direct access to us, where we would be cautiously waiting by the fence, the same fence where we found grandpa on that frosty, winter morning. "Grandma, have you spoken to the morning glories?" I asked.

Chapter Thirty

The moonlight glittered through in a beam of mahogany haze as Chester Potts activated a hollow, ghastly fracture, capturing three of the men from The Mystic Mile, rendering them cataleptic. When they awake hours from not—bearing nothing more than a headache—they will walk away from this night unscathed and unharmed. It will not be the bottom of the pit that they remember the most. No, it will be the moment just before they fell. The hollow layer of earth disintegrating underneath their feet and that silent, slow motion moment of anti-gravity as they descend to the bottom of the dark pit, their stomachs ascending to the top, resting in their throats—false butterflies.

"Charles, I have captured three. I don't see any Lass's." Chester whispered over a night zephyr as I began to white knuckle the fence post that I was standing by—fretfully flaking away—and stripping the loose bark.

"Great job…she is out there, find her." I ordered.

"Enzi, Enid, you stay with me…you four, go down that path." Dr. Spar barked as he pointed towards the path to the left. "You six take Tillie with you and take the path to the right." He barked again, as he pointed towards their selected path. "Don't let anything happen to her!" He shouted as all parties dispersed.

"Dad, what are we doing here?" Enid Rasp asked.

"What do you mean? I am doing this for you…for *all* of you!" He explained.

"It used to feel that way. I used to think that this would help us reach enlightenment…but now…" She said as she cut her off.

"No time now hush and focus. Remember, I want Evonne, you can have *all* the others." He said. "Enzi, when you see it, you take the shot!" He said as he pushed them towards the path down the center, splitting the paths' that the others went down.

"But what about the morning glories?" Enzi asked as Dr. Spar twisted around hurriedly and locked eyes with her like a hawk to its prey.

"YOU SHUT UP about the damn morning glories, it's not real!" He shouted. "NOW GO!"

They gradually began walking down the profoundly wooded path. The heavy substantial smell of pipe tobacco floated overhead as the fireflies speckled the air over the path. Enzi inhaled deeply and became instantly frightened, a proverbial smell, an isolated memory…a forewarning.

"Charles, they are going to come down the middle path to the left. Six men and Tillie are on the path to the right." Ridley Biggs howled as the treetops swayed and the wind whistled through the canopy of the foliage.

"You know what to do…" I began to say, "…Stop the ten men and separate Tillie. Keep her away." I hollered. "Where are the rest of the men?" I asked.

"They are all dotted around the forest; they shouldn't get too close." Antoinette proclaimed self-assuredly.

"Don't let them get too close." I said.

"They would still have to make it through the twinkling, crimson mine field of your grandpa and I…" She said reassuringly.

"Mom, Marla…fall back to the house. Charles, stay here with me."
I said as they recede to the protection behind the vines and blooms
provided by grandma. Charles stepped forward and stood next to me
at the fence line.

"You know, it's funny…" Charles began to say as he looked out
over the strawberry fields. "…It's beautiful but so daunting to look
at." He said. I reached down and grabbed his hand, feeling his
warmth.

"It's less daunting with you next to me…" I said as I smiled, "…Be
ready for anything."

Chester and Ridley handled most of the bulk; seeing as how
they had the furthest reach.

"I don't like this…it's too easy…" One of The Mystic Mile member
said as Tillie trounced close by in their shadows. "…I don't like the
way these trees look, man…" another member said.

"This place…" Tillie began to say, "…is alive. I grew up in these
forests."

"Don't listen to her. She is lying. Trying to distract us so she can leave just like Raven did." The biggest Mystic Mile member said loudly. He was the man with hair the color of combustion and skin that was fish belly white, almost lucid. Tillie unexpectedly inhaled a memorable smell: morning glories.

"Grandma?" She asked as she looked up to see a coverlet of morning glories overhead. The Mystic Mile members all stopped to turn and look at Tillie. "I'm sorry for everything…" She said as he quickly walked up to her, grabbing her by the nape of her neck.

"What the hell—" A man shouted as he vanished. All the men began to get frenetic as they all huddled closer together but still fanned out in every direction. A perfect three-sixty.

"HE WAS JUST HERE—" Another screamed. Another pitfall.

"What is going on? What did you do?!" He screamed as he lunged at Tillie. Grandma dropped her coverlet of vines and blooms ensnaring him.

"Run to the house Tillie, DON'T STOP!" Grandma shouted. Tillie looked back one final time. No Mystic Mile members were in sight, all had vanished below the ground and were replaced by nothing more than puffs of mahogany fog.

"Poodle, Tillie is on her way." Grandma shouted. I Looked back at mom as she stood next to the copper sink next to the open window.

"Mom, Tillie is on her way!" I listened to the howl of the wind over the treetops and then looked over at Charles. "Six more men down." I said to him.

The damp, humid air created pockets of sweat in my palms that collected remnants and particles of dead trees—the fence post that I was holding onto. The bushes near the center path began to rustle as my eyes went wide—like a deer in headlights—and vigilant. Time seemed to slow as Dr. Spar, Enid Rasp and Enzi stepped out from behind the trees and stood there, compellingly. There was a portentous, dark shroud which seemed to summarize all of them.

Chapter Thirty-One

I gradually awoke to the stench of bleach, hand sanitizer and the cold synthetic tubes which fed my lungs the little bit of life that I had been clinging too for God only knows how long.

"Where am I?" I whispered. My throat was the Mojave Desert, desperate for moisture. I dry swallowed which caused me to gag and, as I Ran my fingers across my lips, I Felt that they were just as dry as my throat. "Death Valley…" I throatily whispered. I stared at all the tubes, lines and wires that were running in and out of my body.

"Nurse…" I tried to scream, but my words were abridged to near silence. I pushed the red button to page the nurse and then I began to cry. I wasn't crying because I was in the hospital, I was crying because there was absolutely no colors, aside from the pocket of blood smeared and trapped underneath the clear medical tape which fastened my IV to my left forearm.

"…NURSE!" I managed to scream, as loud as my body would authorize, as mom, who was down the hall getting coffee, heard and ran into my room.

"Charles! Nurse…he's awake, get the doctor!" She hollered as she rushed to my bed side.

I tried to sit myself up in the hospital bed that I was laying in and then I felt it, a razor-sharp pain in my abdomen—like a knife trying to force its way out from the inside. It was mind numbingly painful and it instantly gave me a splitting headache. I looked down and noticed a red circle—the color of Antoinette Denos—expanding in diameter.

"Oh dear, you broke open the stitches…" Mom began to say.
"…Just lie down and relax. Don't try to sit up." She said as one doctor and two nurses walked into the room dressed in the brightest white I had ever seen. "…He is a little confused…" Mom said as the doctor flashed a light in my eyes, checking for my pupil's dilation.

"Charles," The doctor began to lightly say, "…Do you know where you are?" He asked.

"Water…" I responded as the nurse gave me a cup of water from the sink. The water instantly massaged away all the dryness as I sighed in relief. "My throat thanks you." I said through a half-cocked smile.

"How do you feel?" The doctor asked.

"How long was I out? My stomach hurts and I have a headache." I said as I looked at mom. The nurse gave me Tylenol and fixed my stitching as the other nurse set me up on a morphine drip. The doctor gave me a once over and looked over at mom with a rushed look in his eyes as his beeper went off.

"To the O.R. I go. I'll be back to check on him during my next rounds." He said as he clicked his pen and left the room. The other two nurses finished what they were doing and followed suit.

"Honey, you're crying. Are you in pain?" She asked. I looked at her blurry silhouette, thankful for the blue jeans and lavender shirt that she wore.

"It's too white in here…how long was I out?" I asked. She looked around the room and silently agreed as Charles appeared in the doorway with a bouquet of flowers in his hands.

"You have been out for four days. These are from me and Ripp." He said as he put them on the bedside table and then brushed my hair out of my face.

I peeled off the oxygen tube and let gravity take it to the floor. I stared, fixated on the way that it laid on the cold linoleum floor. Like that night when I accidentally yanked the lamp off the side table. The way grandma's oxygen tube rested on the ground in her bedroom as she turned the color of volcanic ash. I will always remember what that looked like. It's been burned into my memories.

"What happened?" I asked as Charles opened the hospital window, letting in a gentle breeze.

"Well..." He began to say as he walked over to me and sat on the bed, "...What is the last thing you remember?" I looked at him and then closed my eyes.

"A wave of crimson and a million lightning bugs." I said.

"Good, what else?" He asked.

"The smells. Sweet peas, strawberry fields, morning glories and pipe tobacco. Oh, and gun powder." I said as I began to list off everything I could remember.

"Go back further...focus..." He said. I was too drained to dispute so I obeyed him as I closed my eyes once more.

Dr. Spar and Enzi stood ten feet in front of me. Enid Rasp ran off into the thicket after being swarmed by grandpa and Antoinette.

"Enzi...take the shot!" Dr. Spar shouted. "TAKE THE SHOT!" Enzi began to cry as she hesitated, halfheartedly holding the handgun with both hands, shaking like the leaves in fall. "No bride of mine will disobey me..." He shouted as he pulled a gun out of his waistband and aimed at the back of Enzi's head. Her eyes widened as the cold steel from the barrel of his gun pressed firmly against the back of her skull. I looked at her and saw her as she was when she was but a child, scared of the monsters in her closet. It was at that exact moment that I didn't even care anymore what horrible things Enzi had done which led up to this very moment, I had to protect my little sister once more from the monsters in her closet. I knew that the only way that I would survive—that we would survive the night—was to let her shoot me and just hope that she didn't hit any major organs.

"If you don't take the shot…" Dr. Spar whispered as he pressed his body up against Enzi's and pressed the gun harder against Enzi's head.

"Enzi…" I said loudly as I grabbed the bottom of my shirt and lifted it up to my neck, "…It's okay. Take the shot." She looked at me as tears began to surge down her face. "TAKE IT!" I Screamed as she closed her eyes and slowly squeezed the trigger. The bullet hit me in the stomach, and I blacked out from the pain and blood loss. Enzi fell to her knees—crying hysterically—feeling guilty that all her choices had led to this conclusion.

I opened my eyes and looked at Charles; his fingers were laced through mine.

"What happened to Dr. Spar?" I asked. Mom walked over to me and smiled.

"He found me in the house protecting Tillie. He was about to shoot me, but Marla grabbed the gun off your father hip and shot him." She said.

"And what about all the others?" I asked as I gave them a befuddled but relieved look.

"The others were trapped and eventually released. Enid Rasp got away…we looked for her everywhere." Mom said as she shook her fists in aggravation and fury.

A hasty wave of fatigue hit me like a tidal wave as the morphine drip began to take away my thoughts and replace them with nothing but blur. "VISITING HOURS ARE NOW OVER." A generic but gentle voice announced over the hospital's PA system. Mom and Charles hugged and kissed me and then took their leave, promising to come back the next day. I lay there, alone, my eyelids heavy like two anchors dropped in the sea, as a nurse came in.

"That morphine kick in yet?" She asked, her voice cacophonously proverbial. I forced my eyes open, combating remedial sleep.

"Hay yellow hair…" I said as she placed her elongated, emaciated finger over my lips.

"You ruined everything…" She said. "…Did you really think that you would win this? That it's over?" She asked.

"ENID RASP!" I shouted. Sedation had just about entirely taken over my self-control.

"…This isn't over, it has just begun. You and your family will pay!" She shouted as I fell into an unfathomable slumber, hypnotized by her narcotic cackle.

As Enid Rasp walked out of the hospital, she peeled off the bright white lab coat that she was wearing and balled it up and tossed it into a dark green trash can. She climbed into a raven black sport utility vehicle; tint as dark as night. As the vehicle drove off, the low grumble from all eight cylinders—so unforgettable and distressing—floated on the air and danced around my room as I lay there, in my almost all white room, medically unconscious but sleeping peacefully.

Please subscribe to www.calsherwoodbooks.com and be on the lookout for my new novel: The Cicada Tree.

Thank you for reading and I hope you enjoyed the adventure.

Made in the USA
Monee, IL
24 July 2022